I0581004

Sandhill Island 1975

Joanne Van Kool

Sandhill Island 1975

Sandhill Island 1975 was inspired by John Sinclair,
who saved Fraser island from sand mining.

Sandhill Island 1975
ISBN 978 1 76109 248 0
Copyright © text Joanne Van Kool 2022
Cover image: Brenda Eldridge

First published 2022 by
GINNINDERRA PRESS
PO Box 3461 Port Adelaide 5015
www.ginninderrapress.com.au

1

The lorikeets screeched and darted among the trees. Flashes of green and red.

Jim sniffed the air. Early morning, but already warm. Outside his shack, he stood for a while. Felt his bones right themselves after a night's sleep. Jeez, he was getting old. It had crept up on him. A darkening shadow crawling into his being. Nothing he could do about it but he resented it.

He sat on an upturned pot and reached into his trouser pocket. A packet of tobacco and papers. He had been told to stop but he didn't see why he should. Been puffing away for sixty years. More. He was still alive even if he was old and his roll-your-owns were a part of his life.

The smoke writhed up through the trees that were sentinels around his hut. He stared at a spider's web, glistening with diamonds of dew. It hung between a tall pandanus palm and a scribbly gum sapling. The spider nowhere to be seen. No doubt a bird had swooped, although the web was intact. Amazing geometry.

The place smelt of rotting vegetation. It was damp down in the folds of the sandhills. Life decayed here but new life was spawned. It pleased him to feel part of it.

A fly settled on his beard. He brushed it off. Stood to go inside under the corrugated-iron roof and through the hanging hessian that constituted a door.

His water container yielded the necessary for a pot of coffee. That smell drowned all others so he felt really alive again.

A half-finished painting stood on an easel under the improvised skylight he'd constructed in the iron roof. As he drank his coffee, he gazed at the painting critically. Probably end up like some of the others, nailed onto the ceiling to keep out the wet. But this one might just be okay. Always that kind of hope.

He emptied his cup. Looked into its depths. Pity. The coffee had allowed him procrastination time. No excuse now.

He rolled another cigarette. Pulled a brush from the stack in the old jam tin. More red. He could see that now. He mixed a colour and puddled in the oil. He tried a stroke where he thought it was needed. Tentatively at first, then with increasing energy, he became absorbed. His cigarette was forgotten, dropped, shrivelled and dead. The end where his lips had been was still damp from his spit. Hours later, it had dried out into a brown colour.

Time didn't matter. Nobody to call or remind him. Suited him fine. At three, he stood back to have another look. Better maybe. Still wasn't sure. He needed a break. Felt suddenly hungry.

The bread bin yielded a half loaf in a bright-coloured wrapper. He sniffed the contents. Shit! It smelt mouldy. The price one paid for living in the semi-tropics. Now he'd have to go into town to buy food. Bugger it!

His boat was down on the island's coast-side beach where he'd left it, dragged up beyond the high-water mark. Down here, the smell of salt water and mangrove swamp took over. There was only this small area of sand that could be called a beach.

Now it was quite hot. He shed his T-shirt and dragged the boat over the sand. He inserted the rowlocks and pulled the slightly chewed-looking oars from the bottom.

Didn't take him all that long to row across to the little wharf at the end of Sandpiper Bay, where the water was protected from the ocean swells by Sandhill Island. He'd left his ute at the wharf. Stinking hot inside that, even with the windows down. The steering wheel burned.

He drove to the main street of the small Sandpiper Bay township, heading for the corner grocery shop cum local café. Madge always knew what items he needed. Knew before he did sometimes.

2

Tracy had heard of old Jim several times but hadn't seen him till now. His hair and beard were grey and unkempt and his trousers looked like they'd seen better days. He was skinny and looked very old to her but Madge said he wasn't.

'Jim? He's not old. Least, not real old. Just looks that way. Hard life, I reckon. Don't live a proper kind of life as an artist and he's never done nothin' else, I was told.'

Tracy watched Jim with renewed interest. He looked just how she'd always imagined an artist would look – different, odd. Sometimes their paintings sold for a lot of money but usually only after they were dead.

'Does he sell any of his stuff?' she asked Madge.

'Oh, yeah. Some guy from a gallery down south comes up and takes the old boy's paintin's back in his van. If you could call them paintin's, that is. Don't understand them meself.'

'Why? What are they like?'

'Well, I dunno really. Just lots of paint. Supposed to be trees and stuff or so the bloke from the gallery said.' Madge had only caught a glimpse of one painting and had been disappointed. She'd imagined scenes of the sea and boats. Or the bush below blue skies and fluffy clouds. It was all she'd ever seen on walls or in the local pub. Jim's paintings looked like a lot of lines and circles. Couldn't tell what they were about.

Tracy regularly called into Madge's corner store to buy a small bottle of chocolate milk. She didn't like the smell of stale beer that permeated the pub. So strong, she could taste it. Sometimes, she felt she didn't really fit in as a waitress. Even that was a fancy name for what she was. A kind of general dogsbody. Still, it was a job and her aunt said she should be grateful.

'We've done the right thing by you, Trace. Now you have to start being responsible for yourself. We can't go on forking out.'

There was always the intimation that she'd been a burden. Before she left school, she'd wondered if she might not go south and learn something of use. Cooking, typing. Become a secretary or, more excitingly, a nurse. Many of her peers had done just that. Had escaped and come back only occasionally to see their parents. They seemed to have donned new skins and spoke a different language. So she felt an outsider with them now. She would have loved to have gone with them but it was hard without money to rent somewhere and pay for books and college. Her aunt and uncle certainly wouldn't help her achieve her dreams.

This artist fellow gave her a glimmer of hope that there was another life outside the small town and the farms, like her uncle's, that spread around it. Jim had contacts with that other world, the world she saw in magazines and on television. Her greatest excitement had been as a kid, tagging along with some of the men when they went fishing. They were all much older than she was and knew her uncle. She thought, with some bitterness, that they no doubt felt they were doing her a kindness. These days, she looked forward to Saturday nights when the young blokes from the farms came into town. They brought life into the place. But her aunt and uncle watched over her movements as though she was a kid, so she had to have an excuse to be allowed out after ten o'clock.

'We don't want you getting into no trouble, Trace,' her aunt said and Tracy knew what the word 'trouble' meant for her aunt and uncle.

She had watched Jim carry his bulging bags to his battered ute, throw them in and disappear inside it. The motor revved up and the vehicle departed in a cloud of exhaust smoke and noise.

She knew where he lived. She'd cadge a lift with one of the blokes when he went fishing and get him to let her off on the island. The idea was so exciting. For the rest of the day, she hardly noticed the smell of beer.

3

Steve slung his bulging backpack over one shoulder and headed for the front door.

His mother's voice called from the kitchen, 'Bye, darling.'

He didn't bother to reply.

It was October and the perfumes of spring teased the senses, awakening the ache of unnamed desires. A Madeira vine had grown up seemingly overnight. It hung snake-like across the front path.

Steve peeled it back and ducked under it.

Fuck it! Nothing seemed good about the day. Yet another…

The footpath leading to the station had been eroded by tree roots, exposed and curled like arthritic fingers through the asphalt. His spongy sneakers buckled and twisted their way towards the station steps beside a graffiti-adorned red-brick wall. Everything depressingly the same. Nothing changed. All very well to talk about this being his last year. 'The world will be your oyster, son.' He could only see the darkness of the shell's inside.

Usually, he used the minutes before the train came in to talk to his mates. They would stand in small clusters chatting, laughing over loudly at some crass joke. Hoping the girls would notice them.

This morning he merely grunted 'Hi ya' to one of his mates.

'Bad mood, huh?'

He didn't need to answer. The train came closer, leering into the station. Steve heaved his backpack into a carriage. He sat on one of the sideways seats near the doors. The others had got the message. They straggled on behind him and went upstairs. He could hear their loud voices and laughter. Didn't want to be one of them this morning.

He stared out at the backyards of houses that flashed past without seeing them. He went over the night before.

His father's face looming larger than ever, the eyes bulging, the knots of veins on the throat. 'You slack-arsed little shit.'

His mother's voice, 'Kev, just cool it a bit.'

'Cool it! With a report card like this?' Back at his son. 'You coulda been anything you wanted, done anything. If you'd just got your finger out, for five bloody minutes.'

Steve's silence apparently further inflamed his old man. 'Not a thing you've done without. Not one bloody thing. You've had it all, holidays overseas, swimming pool, anything you've ever wanted. Busted my guts to give you the best of everything…' A moment's pause to regroup, gather strength. 'And what do I get in return?' Derisive laugh. 'Bloody Cs. Nothing but bloody Cs.'

'He did get one B-plus.' His mother's voice. Not like her to be protective. Maybe she thought the old man might have a coronary. He looked this moment as though he could. Funny really. Objectively. Wouldn't be so funny if that actually happened.

'Yeah. And what for? That one B-plus? Bloody art. For Christ's sake!'

The report card was thrust under Steve's nose as his father seemed to make a huge effort to control himself.

The voice dropped half an octave, tight with suppressed fury. 'Well, you've got just one more term to get it all together, son.' He turned away for a second and then back again. 'I'm telling you only this once and you'd better get it into your head. You'll want to improve or that's it. Out the door. Find yourself something to do. Discover what real work is.'

The sound of a car interrupted the vitriol.

'That'll be Jim and Betty.' His mother almost ran to the window overlooking the driveway. 'Hi!' she called, waving. 'Come on up.'

Now he could escape. Go to his room.

Below his bedroom, he could hear them on the back deck. Talking, laughing, the clink of glasses. He wouldn't go down. Even when his mother came up to tell him food was being dished up, he didn't respond. Only after the plates had been stacked and the foursome were lolling in their chairs outside, did he venture into the kitchen. He collected a piece of steak and a few leftover veg. His father's back was toward him. His mother noticed his presence but clearly decided it was better to ignore him. Keep it cool, she would have said. And who, Steve thought bitterly, would want friends to witness a domestic squabble?

In his room, he ate and then lay on his bed. Stared up at the ceiling. Could he have done any better? Course he could. Deep down he knew that. He was good at the deep down. Deep down, he'd always known that Sarah would end the relationship. He hadn't been her first but she'd been his. It was over now but he hadn't totally lost out. His muscles felt firmer, his masculinity was still intact. Better really. He'd just felt angry for allowing it to get to him. Now he sometimes went over it, in a dispassionate kind of objective way. It had been a pretty good experience, he reckoned. Exciting, and she'd seemed to like it which was a real turn on. Now it was over. He wondered if it had made him depressed. That was a scary idea. Depression. How did one know if one was depressed? His friend Garry hadn't seemed depressed. He'd always laughed at things. Then he'd tried to top himself. Was still in hospital. So he obviously had been depressed. Deep down.

When the train arrived at its destination, the other boys crashed down the stairs, laughing loudly. He sat back in his seat. As the doors closed, he saw one of them glance back, then nudge another. They both looked questioningly at him for a second before turning back to laugh.

He wasn't going to go to school this morning. That much he'd already decided. Last night, in fact. He had a half-formed plan although maybe he'd change his mind.

At Hornsby, he got off and walked to the nearby shopping centre. There was a ten-dollar note in his wallet. He ordered a Coke and sat at one of the small tables in the mall. Rifling through his backpack, he retrieved his bank book. Not even a hundred dollars. The last deposit was when he must have been in Year Ten. Hadn't bothered with school deposits since.

Still, it was enough to take him somewhere. After his Coke, he went to find a Commonwealth Bank, where he drew out all but twenty dollars. Enough to keep the account ticking. He returned to the station to examine the timetables and posters and settled on a place he'd never heard of. On the coast, the map suggested. Might be cheaper to travel by bus but the train was due in soon. He bought a ticket and sat on the designated platform to wait.

The journey took less time than he'd imagined and he was surprised when the Sandpiper Bay sign on the platform announced his arrival. He grabbed his backpack. Jumped down into the heat and cicadas.

Only other passengers to get out were an elderly couple who were immediately seized by enthusiastic friends. Steve took a moment or two to look for directions.

No doubt all hell had broken loose at home. The police'd probably come looking for him. Couldn't make him go home, could they? He was almost eighteen. Next month, he would be. Defiance burnt red within him but money was a worry. If he had a job, there would be no need for him to go back. Not for a while anyway. Bugger university.

It was only a short walk into the small town. Wide street, angle parking. Not much sign of life. A truck was parked outside a hardware shop and two men were tying down a toilet in the tray. Shopfronts straggled down the street then gave way to houses. On stilts for the most part, with timber blinds festooning open verandas.

A man sat on the steps of one of the houses. He was smoking a cigarette and staring into space. Someone spoke to him from inside and he turned his head. 'Didn't touch it, I tell you.' He sounded annoyed.

Steve turned and walked back to the milk bar cum general store he'd seen. He bought a pie and sauce.

The woman behind the counter was elderly and large.

'Is there a backpackers around here?'

'Nah,' she said, peering at him with button-like eyes. 'There's a kinda boarding house place just down the end of the street but. Cheap rooms.'

He found the boarding house wedged between two old rust-coloured houses on stilts. It had the words 'Sandpiper Bay Hostel' written on a sign near the front door. It was a one-storey place of fibro construction, painted pale green with a yellowy cream colour around the windows. Inside, it was dark and smelt of onions and cigarette tobacco.

An old man just inside the door, sitting reading a newspaper, went behind a 'Staff Only' door, returning with a key that he handed to Steve. 'Seven dollars a night,' he said. Room's out the back.'

Steve pulled out his wallet and handed over the required sum.

The man's eyes ran over him before pocketing the money. 'Towels on the bed near the door,' he said, turning back to his newspaper.

At the end of the passage, an open door revealed a dormitory. Four beds, clearly none of them currently slept in. Next door was the loo and a couple of showers.

He dumped his backpack and went back out, passing the man with the newspaper, who didn't look up.

It was pleasantly warm in the sun, too warm to hurry. Nobody seemed to do anything in a rush round here anyway.

4

After she got off her bike and put it in the rack, Tracy pulled her skirt down. She knew it was too short for Bert's liking but maybe he'd be too busy to notice. Her uncle hadn't noticed, or he'd have said.

In the kitchen, which stank of stale beer, she picked up a rag to wipe down the red formica tables on the veranda. The pub was always quiet at this time of the day. Even Bert was absent. Talkative with customers, he was laconic when nobody much was around. She heard the late morning train arrive at the station. The railway line ran inland from the town. The train stopped for a few minutes before the sound disappeared into the distance.

The kitchen cloth felt slimy but there wasn't another. She slapped it down on a table, wiping off the crumbs, some sticking to the rag and others falling to the floor.

She returned the cloth to the kitchen and got out the broom.

Going out onto the enclosed veranda, she saw someone coming towards the front. Hard to make out who it was through the canopy of shrubs and climbers. She began the daily sweep of the cement floor. Later it would be hosed. That was Bert's job.

Although there were no customers at this time, the front door was ajar. She heard it pushed open so went back into the bar to look.

'Hi!' A young man, really young, stood silhouetted in the doorway, peering into the glow.

'Can I help you?' Tracy asked.

'Just wondered if there was a job going.'

Even though he was quite tall and looked strong, there was something uncertain about him.

'Not that I know of.'

He turned to go.

'But if you come back later, I can ask the boss. He'll be around soon.'

'Okay.' He smiled and she noticed the even white teeth. 'Thanks.'

Definitely not a local.

He went out. She returned to her sweeping.

At two, there were the usual sounds of the truck unloading the metal beer barrels. The thump and roll of them down the laneway out the back. Men's voices rising like the heat of the day. The clink of the cash register.

'See ya next Wednesday.' Bert's voice. 'Today's a warm bugger.'

'Good fer business but,' Sam, the delivery guy, said.

Tracy went into the bar as Sam was putting the money into his wallet.

'Well, if it isn't me favourite girl,' he said. Then he chuckled and turned to Bert. 'She's got great legs goin all the way up to her bum.'

'That skirt's a bit short,' Bert noted. 'Don't do to look cheap, Tracy.'

'Aw, she's not cheap, Bert. Just a good-lookin' girl.'

'Yeah…well.'

Tracy smiled at Sam and then busied herself until he'd gone. 'Young bloke came in looking for a job,' she said casually. 'Looked strong.'

'Caught your fancy, did he?'

'Na. Too young for me. Just thought you might have something.'

'Nothin' right now. Should go down to the timber yard. Might be somethin' down there.'

Shortly after two-thirty, the guy came hesitantly into the public bar.

Tracy had been watching for him. 'Boss said try the timber yard,' she said.

'Someone else said that.' He had stubble on his chin. 'I'll give it a go.' He grinned.

Still wet behind the ears, she thought.

'Thanks for asking.' He turned to go.

She stood for a minute to watch him walk down the road, wondered where he'd come from, how he'd get on. Then she shrugged, wiped down the bench and replaced the mats emblazoned with the Tooheys brand. None of her bloody business. It was her early finish day and she had plans.

At three, she yanked her bike from the rack and, instead of going home to the farm, pedalled off towards the wharf.

There were signs of life on the jetty and, when she got off her bike and looked down, she saw the familiar figure of old man Custer bent over the boat's motor. Andy Pedersen, his usual fishing mate, was sorting through some tackle. Custer was probably over eighty but a kind old bugger.

'Can I come for a ride?' she asked and smiled, hoping that would do the trick.

'Keen on fishing suddenly?' Custer asked.

Andy was short and wiry, with long streaky hair and a rat-like face. She'd never liked him, but Custer owned the boat and she felt safe with him.

'Na. Just want a hitch to Sandhill. Not the surf beach. Just the one nearest.'

'Wha for?'

'To see a man about a bone.'

'Oh, I get it. A feller. None of my business.'

'You said it.'

A pause for three seconds while he thought. Then Custer spat into the water. 'Okay. Hop in.'

He started the motor, the boat pulling away from the jetty. Once clear, Custer pushed in the throttle so the vessel shot over the water, leaving a white trail. The noise of the motor was too loud for small talk.

When they arrived at Sandhill's little sandy beach, the motor was killed and Tracy leapt over into the shallow water, cold against her legs.

She waded to the beach and looked back. 'Thanks,' she called. 'See ya.'

'Got ter be back at six, Trace,' Custer said. 'Want us ter pick you up?'

She'd have to get back somehow. 'Thanks. I'll be here.'

The boat motor revved and faded and became a dark shape in the distance.

Tracy walked up the beach to a parting of the bush. A sort of track. Ferns and grasses, crushed and brown.

The trees and low scrub became increasingly dense. The heat lay heavily around her and the noise of cicadas in the gloom gave the place an eeriness.

Suddenly she saw it. The shack rose up like a mound of flotsam.

She was excited and a little scared now, but she walked towards it. Did someone seriously live here? Looked like one of the dilapidated farm sheds at her uncle's place. The structure was supported by timber posts and the walls seemed to largely consist of corrugated iron. The roof was made from palm fronds, draped like thatch. Clearly wasn't totally water proof at times as there were patch-ups of what looked like old timber in several places. There was a large piece of hessian sacking immediately in front of her, obviously the only accessible opening in the structure. She stood outside, feeling shy.

'Hi!' she called. 'Anyone home?'

5

The timber yard wasn't hard to find. On the edge of the small town, at the far end from the sea. Near the entrance, an old bloke was shoving lengths of timber onto shelves and further in, another man was sanding a plank. The place seemed like everywhere else, half asleep.

The old guy turned. 'Yeah?'

'Someone at the pub said you might have some work going.'

'Nah. What gave them that idea?'

'Dunno. I was looking for a job and they said…'

'Not enough for us right now.' He turned back to his pile of timber. 'Sorry, son.'

It wasn't going to be easy. Maybe he didn't look the part. He'd stuffed some jeans and T-shirts into his backpack before he left home, but now he felt he looked too tidy. Too decent.

Feeling awkward and embarrassed by the timber-yard exchange, he walked back to the little café. Red formica tabletops. Western film-star photos on the walls. The air smelt of fresh bread and coffee.

He jingled the few coins left in his pocket. Only a few dollars. Hated to admit it but he knew he was beaten, would have to find a phone to ring home. Let them know where he was. Might be a relief in a way. But he'd have to deal with his father's fury. He thought of his sister, Mandy. Successful Mandy who was always referred to with pride: 'Our daughter's in finance.' Sounded bloody impressive, even to him. But recently he realised being 'in finance' could mean anything from bank teller to stockbroker. She was four years older than Steve and lived another life. Still, she was okay really. Didn't put him down, stuck up for him sometimes when he was in strife with the old man.

He put off the moment of ringing. Would have a coffee first.

'Staying long?' the woman behind the counter asked. 'Not much of a town fer young blokes like you. Be better off in Port. More action there.'

'It's okay.' If she only knew.

He sat at one of the tables. Thought about how it was. Should have thought it through. Prepared things.

There was a sign in the newsagency on the other side of the road. The print was too small to read from this distance. He finished his coffee. No more procrastination. Good word that. Took so long to write that it was self-explanatory.

Jesus! It was really warm now but he left the comforting whirr of the ceiling fan and ambled across the road.

Part-time assistant wanted.
Apply within.

Manna from fucking heaven. A sign maybe.

'Hm…hm.' He coughed and a gnome-like figure appeared from somewhere low behind the counter.

'Can I apply for the job you've got advertised?'

The blue eyes below the bald dome examined him for a second. 'Where you from? Not a local, are you?'

'From down south. I'd like to stay around these parts.' He didn't add the maybe that was on the tip of his tongue.

'I'd prefer a local,' the guy said. 'Still, I'll give you a trial run. Girl I had has gone off for a few months. Pregnant.' He gave a disgusted sort of chuckle. 'Name's Joe by the way. Joe Fisher.'

'Steve Hastings. When can I start?'

'Four today, if you can. Open till six and it can get busy in the last couple of hours. Eighteen, are you, Steve?'

'Yep.'

'Two dollars an hour. Probly six hours a day, 'cept Sunday of course. OK?'

'Sure.' He'd manage to live on that money…somehow. 'See you then.'

Steve thought, Bet he doesn't think I'll turn up.

Back at the hostel, he pushed open a door onto a concrete yard out the back where someone was whistling.

'Need to stay here another night or two. Okay?'

The same old man wearing overalls was bending over a garbage bin. He stood when Steve spoke. 'Last bloody lot must've drunk the pub dry,' he said.' Bin's full of empties.' He focused on Steve. 'Cash up front each night but.'

'Each evening. Okay? Job at the newsagency. Don't get paid till six.'

The man grunted.

He had to fill in time. He decided he'd wander beyond the town in the other direction. The noise of the cicadas was deafening. The few shops were set close to the footpaths of the street to allow angle parking. Two people strolled in the shade of the shop awnings. The heat of the day must have driven everyone else indoors. It was as though people were asleep. Or dead. The houses, weatherboard or fibro, straggled further apart. A caravan park with a toilet block had two long-time immobile caravans. Wheels that had sunk into the soil were now overgrown with weeds and grass. One or two newer vans sat conspicuously shiny at the other end of the park. Steve thought it looked as though their owners wanted to make it clear to the permanent residents that they were genuine travellers, not caravan park layabouts. Boats and surfboards, along with washing strung out over grassy spots, gave the place a sense of life, however transitory. In the far distance, the sea spread its gaping blue, meeting the almost cloudless sky on the invisible horizon.

He breathed in deeply, feeling the clench of his guts, savouring the moment.

A couple of trucks rumbled past, men wearing battered hats crouched over steering wheels, intent on the day. He might remember the moment down the track. I am a camera. Click, click!

Logic. That was what was needed. Like essays. The logical progression of an argument. Leave aside the fact the whole barmy idea hadn't been based on logic. Right now, in this strange environment, he felt disorientated, nothing to hang on to. He should be still at school. Finishing his education. Going on to university like his father wanted. Doing what? Nothing had ever appealed. Only art. That had grabbed him in some strange way and he found he was quite good at it. He liked the feel of charcoal on paper, the slither of black lines on white. His first foray into paints had opened something inside him. He couldn't put his finger on it, knew only that he wanted more.

Now he tried to sort his thoughts. What was he doing? Why had he come here? He should have gone somewhere bigger, where there might be more work, more people his own age.

But why not here? The place had stuck out on the map.

Money was the problem. But the hostel was all right. Bed as hard as goat shit but the WC and shower were okay. At the moment, he could even crap with the door open if he wanted. He wondered when the three other beds had last been slept in. It might have been good to have had some company. Still, at the moment he could leave the light on at night if he wanted to read. Read what? He remembered the paperbacks he'd glanced at in the newsagency. Muscled men and big-tit girls on the covers. Appealing. Could buy one of them. Maybe at a discount. His watch showed five minutes to four. Shit! He walked briskly to the newsagency.

'You're back, then.'

No, I'm a bloody mirage, Steve thought, but said, 'You said four o'clock, didn't you?'

'Now then, the lottery tickets are on the side here and the magazines need to be put on the rack over there.'

Sure enough, as predicted, there was a steady trickle of people. No time to dwell on things, worry about money or the future.

At six o'clock, Joe went outside to pull in the headline stands. 'Closing time,' he said. 'So where you staying?'

'Hostel.'

'Be gone next week, I suppose?'

'Hope not.'

Joe went to the till and handed Steve four dollars. 'Midday tomorrow, then? I need a break around that time.'

Steve pocketed the money. With what he'd got, he'd be able to pay for the room.

But the man wasn't around, so Steve walked down to the little supermarket and bought two apples. He thought about a tin of soup but there didn't seem to be anything at the hostel to cook it in so he went back to the café and bought some hot chips before heading back to the dorm. Sitting on the lower bunk bed, he felt suddenly alone and more than a little scared. Tomorrow at midday. Focus on that. Still, there was a lot of time to kill between now and then.

6

For a few seconds, it seemed as though there was nobody there. Tracy wondered if she should call out again. Then there was a sort of scuffle before the hessian cover was lifted. A pair of rheumy blue eyes stared out.

'Yeah?' His beard was almost matted and he smelt, not dirty, but rather like the earth.

'Hi. I'm Tracy.' She wondered what else she could say that wouldn't sound rude.

'I'm Jim.' His lips suggested a smile.

They stood surveying each other for what seemed to her like an age.

Finally, it was as though he came to a decision and pulled the hessian to one side. 'Most people go to the beach on the ocean side of the island. Fishing and surfing there. But now you're here, you'd better come in.'

'I didn't wanna be rude,' she said as she passed him at the entry.

'Just curious, were you?' He dropped the hessian again and followed her as she gazed about the place.'

She was curious but also weirdly excited. At first appearance, it was a muddle of objects piled one on top of another, rather like a charity jumble sale as Tracy imagined them to be. On closer inspection, she saw a half-finished painting on an easel on an ancient and grubby sort of rug in the centre of the room. In one corner of the space, there appeared to be a bed surrounded by cupboards and shelves piled high with books and papers. There was a lamp suspended from a hook over a table that had three legs, another pile of books substituting for its fourth.

Oh my God, she thought, but all she said was, 'I heard you're an artist.'

'Dangerous to listen to others,' he said. Their eyes met.

She went to stand in front of the easel, stared at the painting perched on it. Contorted figures in browns and greys. Not anything like she'd imagined.

'Not what you expected?' He must have read her thoughts.

Turning to look at him, she felt shy and ignorant. His ill-fitting trousers were held up by pyjama cord and his beard held bits of fluff but there was a knowingness about him. A kind of ancient wisdom. Her sense of bravado had evaporated.

'I never learnt art,' she said. 'So I can't...'

'Learning is only the half of it,' he spoke over her. 'It's the feeling that makes it happen...or not.'

'Oh.' She didn't know what else to say.

There were moments of silence as he stared at the painting and she tried not to stare at him.

'I'm sorry. I shouldn'ta come,' she said.

He turned back to her, eyed her for a moment. 'You'd make a good portrait,' he said.

She was about to laugh but saw he wasn't making fun. 'Oh, I...I work at the pub,' she said, non sequitur.

'All the time?'

'Today's my half day. Came over with Custer. He's gunna take me back so I gotta be at the beach. Custer's a good guy but I don't like his mate, Andy.' The words tumbled. 'Sorry, I didn't mean to...'

He picked up his paint-filled board and pulled a brush from the tin. He wasn't listening to her any more, seemed unaware she was there. He ran a line of grey paint over one of the contorted figures. She sensed she didn't exist but was not at all upset. In fact, it was as though she had been encompassed within this different, set-apart world and she wished she could retain it. That if she moved, it would end.

At last, she went towards the door as silently as she could.

'Come again,' he said without turning.

'Could I?' She paused in surprise.

He turned now to look at her over his shoulder. Gave her a half smile. 'Don't usually like visitors, prefer my own company. Glad you came, though,' he said, before turning back to his work.

She hugged the feeling of exhilaration to herself as she walked back to the beach. She'd have ages to wait now but it didn't matter. There was a piece of twisted driftwood that had been washed ashore so she sat leaning against it, staring out into the blue. She picked up a pebble and doodled on the sand beside her. It's the feeling, he'd said. She smiled to herself. Funny old bugger.

When Custer returned, she took off her sandals and waded out to the boat. He said nothing, just grunted as she swung up and over the gunwale.

Andy sat opposite her, his eyes on her face. 'Good, was he?' he asked.

'Dunno what you mean,' she said. Looking ahead, she avoided his gaze.

He chuckled softly. 'I'll bet you do.'

'Leave her be, Andy,' Custer said, before letting out the throttle.

All the way back, Tracy felt Andy's eyes on her, and when she reached for the ladder to take her back up to the jetty, he held out his hand to help her.

She ignored him, saying, 'Thanks, Custer.'

Andy and Custer were part of her everyday world. She'd just discovered another world and she hugged the thought to herself as she cycled home.

7

'Where the hell are you?' His father's voice. 'Your mother's sick with worry.'

There was a scuffling sound. Steve imagined his mother grabbing the phone.

'Steve, darling!' There was a sob. 'I've been desperate. We both have. We need you to come home. You're so near the end of your school life now…we both know you…'

Another scuffle.

This time his father's voice. 'Your mother says all boys of your age are searching for something different. But I know what it is,' the anger again, 'it's just bloody selfishness. You've got no idea, not a bloody clue what life is all about. Best you come home right now, my boy.' The veins would be standing out on the old man's neck. 'Right now, d'you hear? You get on a train or a bus or whatever and you come straight on back here. I won't answer for the consequences if…'

'Your father doesn't know what he's saying, Steve.' His mother must be on the other line now. 'He's so terribly upset.'

'After all I've done for you, you…you…' his father struggled to be calm. 'So where are you?'

Funny, only now was the old man actually starting to ask sensible questions.

'I'm up the coast. Working in a newsagency. Discovering what life is all about.'

'I suppose you realise we've notified the police. They'll be out looking for you.'

'Dad, I'm not ready to come home yet.'

There was silence on the other end as his parents absorbed his words.

'I've got things to do here.'

'Like what?'

Steve wasn't about to admit the truth. 'All kinds of things. It's all go in this town.' When he was a kid, he would have expected a pimple to grow on his tongue for that fib.

'Are you eating properly?' His mother's tearful voice cut in. 'Where are you staying?'

'I'm fine, Mum.' He seriously didn't want her to worry. 'I'm okay… really.' It was doubtless a waste of time to suggest the police should be told that he had been found.

'You might give some thought to the money I've spent on your education.'

Steve inwardly sighed.

'So close to university and a career of your choice.'

'Dad, I never wanted to go to university.'

'Well, you never will now. You've successfully made a mess of that.' Another moment's pause. 'So…' Sarcasm always came next. 'What, if I may be so bold as to ask, do you want to do? With your newly acquired great knowledge of the world, how do you imagine your future to be?'

'I just thought I'd play it by ear.'

Renewed rage throbbed down the line. 'Oh, my God! A fucking dropout. Never thought I'd have a useless git for a son.'

'Oh, don't, Bob. He's still our son.'

They were at each other's throats now. It was going around and around.

'I'll ring again,' he said. 'Promise, Mum.' He suddenly felt tears bubble. 'Love you,' he said. 'I'll keep you posted. Promise.'

He leant his head against the wall of the phone booth for a moment. Struggled.

Then he stood up and looked down the street. He'd made contact. Not given in. He was no longer under the control of his father. Could bloody do what he liked. He stepped out of the booth and, feeling a new sense of independent manliness, went into the newsagency. 'Hi, Joe,' he said. 'Not late, am I?'

8

Tracy's evening chore on the farm was to muck out the cow bails and dairy barn. This evening, as she worked, she reflected on how boring her life was. Everything was so…so…the same. Her uncle and aunt had been good to her, taken her on when her parents were killed. But they didn't understand how she craved another life. Farming wasn't what she wanted. Not for the rest of time, anyway. The stench of urine and manure. She tried to blot it out, thinking of the old man on the island. He belonged to another world, interesting, intriguing, and she determined she'd do as he'd said. Go there again. Sometime.

Next morning, Bert sent her out to pick up the local newspaper.

'Bloke last night said a new business of some kind is gunna make us all rich.' Bert gave a dry chuckle. 'Believe it when I see it but do no harm to see if it's mentioned in the news.'

In the newsagency, she recognised the young bloke who'd come looking for a job. He was placing magazines in various racks.

'See you got work then,' she said. Then she turned a radiant smile on Joe. 'He's a good boss, Joe.'

'You coulda had the job, Trace, if you'd applied.'

'Nah. I've got Bert trained now,' she said and laughed.'

'I'll bet you have,' Joe chuckled, then wagged a finger at Steve. 'Don't listen to her. She's a bad influence.'

Mid-morning she went down to Madge's shop to buy a bottle of chocolate milk. The young man was seated at one of the tables just inside the door. He lifted a hand to acknowledge her.

'Hi ya,' she said. 'Lunch? Or have you finished for the day?'

'I don't start till midday, just called in for a moment this morning.'

'And he got you working.'

'I was happy to help for a couple of minutes.'

'Well, aren't you mister good guy?' She laughed and sat in the chair opposite him.

'That's not what my family would call me,' he said.

'You don't get on with your folks, then?' Tracy thought of her aunt and uncle.

'Not really.' Steve didn't want to be drawn on his background, was sorry he'd mentioned the family.

'My parents died in a car crash. When I was a baby. Just got an aunt and uncle. They've been good, I spose. Boring, though.' She drank silently before saying nonchalantly, 'Met an interesting old bloke yesterday but.'

Clearly Steve was expected to be interested. 'Oh yeah. Where d'you find him?'

'On Sandhill.' When he looked mystified, she added, 'Sandhill Island. Out there.' She flapped a hand in the general direction of the sea. 'You can see it if you go to the jetty.'

'Does he live there?'

'In a kinda way,' she said. 'Not in a proper house but. Just a kinda shack.' Tracy shook the bottle, held it up to peer at it and plunged her straw back to suck noisily at the dregs.

'Not many young guys here,' he said. 'Sort of dead, really.'

'You wait till Saturdee. They all come into town then.' She smiled. 'From the farms. Place comes more alive.'

'At the pub?'

'Mostly.' She had a faraway look on her face. 'Had a huge barbie on the beach once. And coupla guys got boats. Go surfing. Out fishing and stuff.'

It didn't sound very exciting to Steve but anything would be better than the last couple of days. The town seemed to consist almost entirely of old people.

Tracy got to her feet. 'Thanks, Madge,' she called out, then, glancing down at Steve, 'Gotta get back to work.' She pulled a stray lock of hair behind one ear. 'Come up the pub later if you like.'

'I don't finish till six.'

She shrugged. 'See ya Saturdee then.'

It was only Thursday and not for the first time, Steve felt adrift with nothing to hold on to. Nothing familiar. Comfortable. He looked at his watch. Only a quarter to eleven.

Madge was looking at him. 'She's a good girl is Trace. Bit rough around the edges, but decent.'

Steve left the milk bar and wandered down towards the beach. He hated to admit it, but he was missing home.

9

Jim sat on the upturned crate watching the smoke from his cigarette float up through the filtered sunlight. He was taking a break from his current project. Rain falling on water. Loved rain. Could smell it coming.

The huge fronds of the king ferns were interspersed with tall native grasses. The odd scribbly gum and, here and there, huge kauri pines rose up as though to shut out the light. He felt at home in this place. No one to annoy him. He'd seen the world, sailed the seas. Now he wanted quiet. Time to recreate the images. To create new ones from this place he called home.

There was a beach further around the island, on the side away from the mainland. People went there a good bit in the summer but didn't bother him. They'd pull their boats up onto the beach near his place. Mostly it was surfers who'd walk the path across to the surfing beach. He'd often find the ashes of a barbecue in the dunes behind the beach. The odd T-shirt left behind, a rubber thong. Nobody camped there or stayed overnight. Wasn't allowed. Not that that would stop some youngsters but it seemed they accepted the rule. They went back to the caravan park on the mainland, or wherever, at dusk.

Snakes could be a nuisance. Once, one slithered in through the hessian. A bloody great python. Not looking for him, though. Just a neighbour checking the place. He'd stayed still until, investigation over, the creature retreated. Oozed out the hut door. Brown snakes were more of a worry, but he didn't kill them. Part of his world, he reckoned. Or rather, he was part of theirs. Sometimes, he wandered to where the track ran to the surfing beach. Trees were denser there, made the place darker. Smelt of pine and rotting foliage. Then it was suddenly, blindingly, wallum heath and beyond that the sand. Bloody miles of it. Undulating reddish yellow. Beyond that the crashing sea. In the sun, it had a beauty of its own. The seabirds swooped and cried. Little scratches of claws dotted the sand. He drew the images in his pad and they haunted him in the night.

Not many dingoes now. Occasionally, he'd hear a howl in the night. Among the other night-time noises. The bush was never silent. Bloody amazing, really.

Funny how that kid arrived at his place. How the hell had she found it? Bit scary that she had. Seemed nice enough. Good bone structure. Hadn't done a portrait in years. Quite like to give it a go again. Oh well, he'd not see her again, most likely.

What the fuck was that? He stood, straining his ears. The sound of a large motor. Bloody tourists disturbing his peace. He stroked his beard as he wandered down to the beach. Voices. Several men.

He padded down the track to the beach. Curious. Three men were walking away from a stink boat. Bloody huge thing, all chrome and white. They had on shorts and the sort of T-shirts that looked expensive. They all wore sunglasses and straw hats. One of them stopped to scoop up a handful of sand.

Another saw Jim. 'Hi ya,' he called. 'Disturbing your fishing?'

'Nah. I live here.'

The three men looked at him.

'Weren't told anyone actually lived here.'

'Well, I do.'

'Is that your dinghy?'

'Yeah, it's mine.'

The conversation seemed to be going nowhere.

'If you've come to surf, you've come to the wrong end of the island.' Jim wanted them gone.

'This is the closest place to bring a boat. No waves.'

'What you here for if it's not a rude question?'

'Just doing a bit of a recce,' one of the men said with a smile. 'For our boss.'

'What's your line then?' There was something cocky about the visitor.

'Mining. Sand mining.'

'None of that around here.' Jim spoke firmly.

'Might be soon, though.' The man smiled again in a patronising kind of way.

'I bloody hope not.' A point had to be made now. 'Spoil the natural habitat.'

The three glanced at each other before one of them said, 'We never do that, mate.'

One of the others said, 'We've got great respect for the environment. Always leave things how we found them.'

Jim was about to say mining never did that but the men had walked past him and along the track.

'See you later,' one of them said over his shoulder before they disappeared.

Jim walked slowly back to his hut. Couldn't settle to anything. Not till they'd gone. Fear simmered. What might this mean? Surely it was just like they said, a look. Nobody would want to mine here? Would they? And anyway, what for?

About an hour later, he heard the men return. He watched silently through the curtain of vines and leaves as they waded out to where their boat rocked gently. Voices burbled but words were indistinguishable. One of them laughed. Then the motor roared and they shot off, leaving a great white surge in the water behind them.

Jim pulled his half bottle of Scotch from the shelf above his bed. He unscrewed the lid and took a generous swig. Felt the familiar burn in his throat. The alcohol surged. He sat on his bed for a long time. Then he shrugged and went outside. The soft orange light of the afternoon sun spoke reassuringly. It wouldn't happen here. Surely not. Fucking couldn't.

He sat on his usual upturned pot and rolled another cigarette. The smoke spiralled up as though nothing had happened. He pulled out his notepad. Gazed at his drawing of the morning. That was real. He'd start working on it tomorrow.

10

The music issuing from the pub on Saturday night was loud. The thump of the drum almost shook the old building. Steve could hear voices and laughter before he reached the door. A strong smell of fried steak and onions.

Inside, the place pulsed with life. Where the hell had they all come from? It was as though this was a different town. The oldies had gone. Disappeared. Only young bodies stood, sat, propped up the bar.

Tracy was pulling the beer. She saw him, waved and grinned. 'Hi ya,' she shouted.

Steve wove his way to her. 'Thought you didn't work nights.'

'Just helping Bert out for a while,' she said. She nodded in the direction of the veranda. 'When the barbie starts, they don't want so much booze. And after that, it's dancing. On a good night, anyway.'

He grinned at Tracy. 'See you when you knock off serving then.'

Steve bought a beer. He turned and looked at those around him. Tight-fitting shirts, flared jeans. Chicks in low-cut blouses.

'Not from these parts?' A young bloke smiled. Slouch hat and elastic sides.

'Nah. Away from the big smoke for a while.'

'Wise move. My old man's got a cattle property, so I'm kinda… like…you know. Good to meet you.' Steve's hand was gripped in a vice. 'Mike.'

'Steve.'

'Where you livin'?'

'Hostel place.'

'You workin'?'

'Newsagent's. Joe's.'

Laconic comments filled in time.

Tracy appeared at Steve's elbow. 'Don't believe a word he says.' She grinned at Mike. 'Where ya been? Haven't see ya for ages.'

'Bin busy. Brandin' the mob.'

'Better get some steak for the barbie or it'll be gone.' She nodded in the direction of the bar.

There was a tray of meat on one end. They each tonged a piece of steak on paper plates. Out in the courtyard, they eventually found spaces on the two already meat-strewn barbecues. Most of the crowd had moved outside and were engaged in loud banter. A far cry from the usual life in the small town.

The music, reasonably subdued till then, now rose in volume. The thudding of the drums and call of the electric guitars must surely have found their way into the homes of the local inhabitants. Tracy was clearly at ease with both the blokes and the girls. Steve was left to cope. He noticed one or two of the girls whispering.

'You new here?' One of them, plump with dimples, had come to stand beside him. She shouted over the din. 'Not seen you before. 'I'm Melissa,' she said and giggled. 'Mel for short, o'course.

'Hi, Mel. Steve.'

Must have already been a rerun of this opening conversation at least ten times. But everyone seemed friendly and the beer was making Steve feel relaxed so he didn't mind.

Tracy came to join him and Mel. Her apron now off revealed a low-cut top above flared blue trousers.

'Hi, Trace.'

The two women took each other in. Noted the clothes, the hair.

'You look good, Trace.'

'Don't look bad yourself.'

They grinned at each other.

'Hey, heard the latest?' Mel's brown eyes sparkled.

'Nah. What's new?'

'They're gunna dig a mine on Sandhill.'

'No. When? Where did you hear that?'

'Some bloke came to talk to my dad. Said it'll be good for the town.'

'Not so good fer the bloke I know who lives there.'

'You mean the old artist?'

'Yeah. Nice old fella.'

'He'll just have to move, I spose.' Mel saw Tracy's expression. 'Come on… He's old, Trace. He won't want to die there all alone.'

'I think he might. He doesn't like people much.'

'How d'you know?'

'I met him.' Tracy was proud of her encounter. 'He lives in a kinda shack. But he's really nice, Mel. Weird, o'course. But nice just the same.'

The crowd was all round them and they had almost to shout.

Then, without warning, a space appeared in their midst. One young guy was squatting, passing a beer bottle between his legs to reach as far forward as he could. The parted crowd urged him on. Eventually, he gave up and stood to let another have a go. Six or so guys had a try. Then another produced a long piece of what looked like cane.

'Limbo. C'mon.'

Steve knew this one. He joined the queue. The chicks were better at it on the whole.

'Go on, Trace,' someone called. 'You can do it.'

The cane kept being lowered by the two blokes who held it. The chicks looked kind of sexy when they got down as low as they could and wriggled their way under the cane.

Steve lined up. Was aware of the groan as he stepped forward. But he knew he could do it.

The cane was really low. He lay back as far as he could. It was lower than anyone else had managed.

'Go on, Trace. You can beat that,' someone shouted and there was loud laughter.

'Nah,' she said. 'Steve's the winner.' She held up Steve's arm like a prize fighter. 'Good on you,' she said.

Voices echoed her words. He felt good. As if he'd really achieved something, though he knew he hadn't.

The dancing began with a couple or two. Soon they were nearly all gyrating, arms in the air, hips thrusting and twisting. Only one or two guys hung at the edges, beers in hand.

Steve pulled Tracy towards him. They watched each other as they moved. She had a great body, arms waving, her head thrown back, laughing. Suddenly some dude came from nowhere, pushed Steve to one side and grabbed at Tracy. She wasn't laughing now. She tried to pull away but he held her hair with one hand, pulled her head back, his mouth on hers.

She broke free for a second. 'Andy!'

But he tightened his hold.

The mood of the crowd changed.

'Leave off.'

'Let her go.'

Steve's fist balled and he struck the bloke from the side. It was enough to break Andy's hold on Tracy. Send him staggering sideways. In a second, he gathered himself, threw a sloppy punch at Steve. But Steve wasn't drunk. Andy was. The crowd stood still. The music was the only sound. Steve was aware of the tension.

'Stop it, Andy,' Tracy shouted. 'Stop it.'

Andy wiped his mouth. Spat. 'Stupid fucking cunt,' he said. Then he gave a twisted, thin-lipped smile. 'You'll keep.'

Hands reached out to haul him through the crowd.

Tracy's face was contorted in fury. She swiped her mouth with the back of her hand, an angry gesture. 'Bastard,' she shouted after the now departed Andy.

Guys he'd not met before seemed genuinely impressed by Steve's bravado.

'Time he got his comeuppance,' said one.

'Shit! You did for him, mate.' Spoken in admiring tones.

'Are you okay?' Steve couldn't think of anything else to say to Tracy. His knuckles burned.

Mel moved to her friend, putting an arm around her and pulling her close. She said scathingly, 'What you think?' She led Tracy through the still silent crowd.

Subdued chat began again, slowly increasing in volume and the music pounded once more.

Steve followed the two women to the door. Outside, Tracy gently pushed Mel away and leant against the door frame.

'What the hell was all that about?' Steve asked.

'I've never liked him…Andy,' she said. 'He thinks I'm easy.'

She was beginning to cry now so Steve put one arm round her in an awkward attempt at comfort. She buried her head into his shirt. He felt strong and protective. He put his other arm round her. Mel gave them a look then disappeared.

After a moment or two, Tracy looked up at him and smiled, the tears wet on her cheeks. 'You can pack a punch,' she sounded admiring.

'He was drunk.'

'Yeah. But he won't take you on again, I reckon.'

'You okay now?'

'I guess. But I don't wanna go back in there. I'll go home, I spose.'

'Will you be safe on your bike?'

'I usually phone my uncle and he comes to get me.' She gave a derisive laugh, 'Doesn't trust me.'

'Where d'you ring him from?'

'There's a phone behind the bar.'

'I could ring him for you, if you like. Save you going back in.'

'Nah. I'd better ring. He'll be really suspicious if you ring.'

Steve followed her inside the door and waited while she went to make the call. One or two people obviously made kind comments as she passed because she nodded and smiled at them. When she came back, they both went outside again.

'Takes him fifteen ta get here.'

'Did you tell him what happened?'

'Nope. And I won't. What he doesn't know won't hurt him. You going back in? Can if you want to. Andy won't be annoying me again for a while. Probly never.'

'I'd rather be sure of that.'

She looked at him for a second. 'Thanks,' she said.

She looked so vulnerable. Steve wanted to kiss her but hesitated. The moment passed.

For a few seconds, they stood in silence. The music thudded behind them. Voices and laughter welled up. The lights from inside made the shadows dance on the street.

She wondered aloud, 'I don't know what'll happen to the artist fella? I guess someone oughta warn him.'

'Maybe he knows.'

'Doubt it. Madge wouldn't say. And he doesn't go there all that often. Doesn't see anybody much. His paintings are weird but he says it's the feeling that has to show to make it good.' She looked at Steve thoughtfully. 'D'ya want to meet him? The old bloke?'

'I dunno.'

'I don't want to go again with Custer. Andy'll probly be with him. If you came, I'd be okay. He wouldn't try anything then.'

'Okay. When d'you want to go?'

'Might cycle over tomorrow. See if they're going fishing. Maybe there'll be someone else anyway. Lotsa blokes go out on weekends. Some of them go to the quiet beach this side of the island but some just stay on their boats. Sure to be someone going.'

'Could be interesting.' Steve wasn't sure he wanted to be involved. 'Where do we meet up?'

'Down at the wharf. Eight thirty. They go out all hours.' She scuffed a pebble with her shoe. Flashed him a grin. 'Come back all hours too. We just have to tag along with whoever.'

'Okay with me,' he said. Sunday might be more exciting than he'd feared.

11

The shriek of birds woke Steve much earlier than he'd intended. Bugger it! He rolled over and closed his eyes again. Then jerked awake. His watch was on the floor by the bed. He reached down to look at it. Shit! Eight o'clock. He'd better get a move on. His clothes were piled on the floor. Hadn't much left that was clean. He'd have to wash some underdaks and Ts. Not now, though. He showered, wondered if he should shave but decided not to. Grinned at himself in the mirror over the basin. Thought he looked okay. A bit of stubble made him feel masculine.

He'd guessed that nothing would be open on Sunday in this town and had bought an extra apple. Pub'd be open later and he could get something to eat then.

It was the usual spring morning. Going to be hot later. The early morning yellow glow had already turned white. Blinding! He was glad he'd brought sunnies.

He walked quickly down to the wharf, where several figures were moving about. When he got close, a few middle-aged blokes were obviously loading gear into boats that bobbed beside the jetty. Milk crates contained jumbles of fishing tackle, lobster pots, rowlocks and ropes. There were a couple of older women but he couldn't see Trace, so he sat on a bollard to eat his apple. Stared out at Humpback. Just looked a mass of green. No sign of life.

He didn't have to wait long.

Steve saw Tracy cycling towards him. She waved.

As she came closer, she grinned. 'Hi ya,' she leant the bike against some lobster pots. 'Prob'ly Custer's not here today. I'll just see who'll maybe take us.'

She stood looking at the boats. Moved to stand nearer to one. 'Got room on board for two more?'

A middle-aged bloke looked up at her. Shielded his eyes to see clearly. 'Where you wanna go?'

'Sandhill for a coupla hours.'

He turned towards the hatch. 'C'n we take the girl and her mate to Sandhill?'

A grey head appeared from below. He looked up. 'Reckon,' he said before disappearing again.

Tracy doing the talking made Steve feel redundant.

'C'mon,' she whispered as she took off her sandals. 'Before they change their minds.'

She turned to put one foot behind her onto the deck, holding on to the jetty. Letting go, she turned again and sat on the side seat. Steve took off his thongs and followed. The boat swayed in the water.

The bloke on deck was screwing on a metal cleat near the tiller. He looked up. 'Other side,' he said.

Steve slid across and smiled at Tracy.

They sat in silence as the men got ready.

The guy from below came up, grinned at them. 'Ready, mate?' he asked the skipper.

'Be too late if we don't go now.'

The motor roared and, after easing away from the jetty, the boat took off.

'The artist's beach?' the man at the tiller yelled above the noise of the engine.

'Fine,' Tracy yelled back.

When they got close, the motor was allowed to idle as the two of them got off and waded towards the shore. The sand was so yellow it was almost orange.

On the beach, Steve put his thongs on again. 'So?' he said.

'Follow me.' Tracy led the way up the track.

The humpy came into view.

'Wow! Far out!'

'Weird, isn't it?'

Steve stood surveying the structure.

Tracy moved to the entrance. 'You there, Jim?' she called out.

The old man eventually appeared. 'Hello again,' he said, half smiling. 'Trace, isn't it?' He looked at Steve. 'Your boyfriend?'

Steve and Tracy exchanged glances.

'Nah, just a friend. His name's Steve. He's from down south.'

'Ah!' Jim pulled back the sacking and motioned them inside. 'Just had breakfast. Still tea in the pot.'

'No, thanks. Just thought we'd see if you're all right.'

'Of course, young don't drink tea.' Jim chuckled. 'No Coke here. Sorry.'

Steve still stood at the entrance, taking it all in.

'Why wouldn't I be all right?'

'There's talk of a mine, a sand mine.'

Jim motioned for her to sit and poured himself a mug of tea. Had he heard her? She sat on a wooden chair that wobbled a bit.

'I thought maybe you'd know. Then again maybe you wouldn't.' She spoke with a rush. 'And anyway, it mightn't happen but if it did you'd prob'ly have to go. The miners would take over and you'd have to leave your house, cos you don't own the land, do you? But maybe you...'

'Just slow down, young lady.' Jim had a soft, rather husky voice.

An old man's voice, Steve thought. Like his grandfather's. He perched on a stool near the table that was piled high with books and papers.

Jim said, 'Nobody's going to make me go. Where did you hear all this anyway?'

'In town. People.'

Jim wagged a finger at her. 'Never believe people.' He smiled. 'Not till they produce evidence.' He wasn't going to tell the girl about the two men. Preferred to blot out that memory. He picked up his pad and a piece of charcoal. 'Now you're here, I can use the opportunity to sketch you. Would you mind? Haven't done a portrait for ages.'

'I don't mind, but a bit boring for Steve,' Tracy said.

'There's lots to see round here. It won't take long. Just a quick scribble. I can make something of it later.'

'I know,' she smiled. 'It's the feeling that matters.'

'Could I try drawing Tracy too?' Steve suddenly felt a compulsion.

Tracy stared at him, surprised.

'I was quite good at art,' he said defiantly.

Jim fussed through the papers and produced a sheet of what looked like butcher's paper. He handed it to Steve and pulled a pencil from the mug nearby. 'There's a board over there near the sink. I think I've got a clip somewhere. You all right on the stool?' Jim was poking about in the muddle on the table, eventually producing a clip. 'Here,' he said.

He turned to Tracy. 'You just sit there like that. Just like you are now.'

He went to perch on an old wooden box in front of her, paused for a moment or two, his head on one side, then the other, before beginning to scribble.

The charcoal slid and squeaked across the paper. It was the only sound in the place for a while.

Outside, the cicadas scratched and a bird screeched. They were an island on an island, Tracy thought. She wanted to scratch her nose but didn't dare. They were suspended in time.

Jim shifted. 'Need a smoke,' he said.

'C'n I move now?'

He didn't answer. Had gone to stand behind Steve. Gazed down at his sketch. 'Not bad,' he said. 'A bit stilted but you've got the idea.'

Steve felt really chuffed but didn't want to show it. 'Only thing I enjoyed at school,' he said.

Jim took Steve's pencil and added a couple of lines. He grunted as he drew as though it was an effort. He stood back then and he and Steve stared at it.

Steve looked up at him. 'Made all the difference, those two lines. Why didn't I see that?'

'Bin at it years,' Jim said. He pulled his tobacco packet from his pocket. 'Never get it just right o'course.' He began rolling a cigarette. 'Not exactly how I see it.'

Steve stood looking at Jim's drawing. 'Far out!' It was like nothing he'd ever seen before. Just a few lines. But it was all there. Captured. Even her expression.

'Enough to paint,' Jim said. 'Rest's in here.' He jabbed his fingers on his head before lighting his cigarette.

Tracy had had enough. 'You haven't said. C'n I move?'

'Course. Sorry.'

'I haven't tried oils much.' Steve was gazing at the tubes and rags on the table.

'Easier than watercolours.' Jim grinned. 'Can't cover up mistakes with watercolours.' He picked up a tube and squeezed out a dob of yellow onto his palette. 'Good base for skin starters.' His cigarette hung from a corner of his bottom lip as though stuck there.

The paint flowed on a section of Tracy's forehead before he added some red and green onto his palette. 'Now I'll add a touch of these.' The colours swirled. 'See? Got to stand back a bit.'

Steve stood beside the old man. Together they surveyed the picture.

'Can't be mean with the paint. Slap it on. If you don't like a bit, you can add another colour. It's all fixable.'

Tracy had been wandering round the room. Now she came to stand near them. Looked at Jim's drawing and then at Steve's. 'Impressive,' she said to Steve and smiled.

But Jim was mixing another colour. Pink and green with a touch of yellow. He began to puddle them together, sucking in his breath as he concentrated. Steve stood watching, mesmerised.

'Think we ought to go,' Tracy said. 'Have to signal someone.'

Steve glanced at her and nodded before turning back to watch Jim. The old man seemed to have forgotten their existence.

'Steve!'

'Yeah.'

'It's time to go. Too late and we'll never got off the place.'

Reluctantly, Steve dragged himself from watching Jim at work. He followed Tracy to the entrance.

'See you, Jim,' she said. 'We'll be back…maybe.'

Jim suddenly awoke to their leaving. He turned, put two fingers to his forehead in a kind of salute. 'See you. Mind you do some more painting.' He watched them leave.

They made their way down to the beach. Scanned the horizon. There was a boat in the distance so Tracy jumped and waved.

'The way you do things here?'

'They all look at Sandhill. Sort of habit, I guess.'

'And they'll come?'

'They will. In a while. When they're ready.'

Even as Tracy spoke, the boat seemed to be coming in their direction.

'Told you,' she said.

They waded out and the boat slowed when it got near. The two guys on board were sunburnt and said nothing as Steve and Tracy threw themselves on to the deck, their feet making wet marks on the timber.

12

Two smart-looking men came into the corner store. In their early fifties. They carried briefcases and looked like the apocryphal used-car salesmen.

Madge handed them cups of coffee in plastic mugs, her eyes running over them. 'Visiting, are you? Nice this time of year.'

The two men glanced at each other.

'Yeah. Just here for a while.'

They wore ties and didn't look like they were on holidays. Madge was curious but didn't want to seem so.

They went to sit at one of her tables near the entrance, speaking in low voices. A magpie strutted past the open door, stood to stare inside for a moment, head on one side, as curious as Madge.

After a few minutes, a third man in shorts and long socks came in. He had a roll of papers under one arm. 'Ready?' he asked. 'The boat's down off the jetty.'

The chairs scraped the floor as the two stood.

'Looks like we're overdressed,' one of them said and laughed.

'You'll be right. Just take your shoes and socks off when we get to the beach.'

Madge went to the door to watch them walk towards the wharf. Then she turned the Open sign to Closed and shut the door before walking to the newsagent's.

'Three blokes,' she laughed, 'could call them the Three Amigos, arrived and gone off to Sandhill. Them miners you heard about, I reckon.'

'Say anything, did they?'

'Not so I could hear. But another bloke said there was a boat down the jetty. D'ya think they're serious? Looked it.'

Joe laughed, 'Could be anything, Madge. There've been a few odd bods around here lately. You know what it can be like in summer. Vans and tents.'

He'd wondered about Steve. Another odd bod. Where had the lad come from? Why Sandpiper Bay? He seemed good value. Worked hard. Didn't complain about doing boring jobs. He'd tried to talk but Steve had shut up like a carnivorous plant. Only thing Joe knew for sure was that he came from Sydney and now lived at the local boarding house, more correctly named a hostel. Joe guessed Steve didn't want to talk about home or his parents. Maybe there'd been some kind of trouble there? Anyway, he felt sure he wasn't about to find out any more. Didn't matter really. Steve worked well, was reliably on time. Polite to the customers. What more could he want?

'But it's not proper summer yet, Joe. An' these blokes weren't from the van park.'

'Well, I wouldn't get excited yet. Could be we'll be in the money but could also be just a couple of guys lookin' to do some fishin'.'

'In suits? With papers all rolled up? Official-lookin' papers?'

'Well, you just watch and see when they come back.' Joe was a bit more interested now. 'Might go to the pub later. Bert'll know what's goin' on.'

It was well into the afternoon before the men returned. Their shirt sleeves were rolled up, ties disappeared. Madge watched them go to a parked Land Rover, throw in the papers, slam the door and drive towards the pub. Safe now for her to close for the night.

In the public bar, the men ordered beers, leant against the counter.

'Warm out there,' Bert commented as he pulled the pints.

'You can say that again.'

'They say it's gunna be a hot summer.' He waited while the men drank, wiped the froth from their lips. 'Come far?'

'Sydney yesterday,' one of them said, a short guy with a big paunch.

'Bugger of a long haul that.' Bert sounded sympathetic. 'Good fishin' round here but.' He paused, waited, wiped the bar top with a damp rag. 'If that's what you come for.'

'Nah. It's not the fishing we're after, mate.' An older guy with a large red nose spoke. 'We're after other things.' He patted his nose with a forefinger. 'Minerals. Bloody money-making minerals.'

'Ah-ha,' Bert made it sound as though he knew all there was to know about such things. 'Dunno if we've got much of that round here.' He suddenly exuded warmth, leant forward. 'Name's Bert. Reckon you blokes know a good venture when you see one.'

'Yeah, well,' the man with shorts and long socks said.

'Be a while till we get it all set up.' Large paunch hitched up his trousers as he spoke. 'We're after mineral sands. Lot of bloody sand on that island. An American company. Our job to look at the place. Size it up. There's another coupla blokes down at the hostel. We're only waiting for the big bosses to give the all clear from the US of A. Then we'll be digging up the bloody minerals by the bucketload. We'd like to take a couple of rooms here at the pub, if that's okay. Start next week. What you charge?'

'Twenty a night. No food.'

'Fine with us.' He winked. 'Don't cost us.' He leant towards the bar and spoke conspiratorially. 'Weird guy living on the island. What's his thing?'

'Jim? Oh, he's all right. Been there a while.' Bert was on familiar ground now. 'An artist. Sells his stuff down south. In the big smoke. Bin all over the world, I hear. Gettin' on now, decided to settle down.' He looked around to make sure they were not being overheard. 'Built his place with his own hands.' He chuckled. 'Bit of a humpy, I hear.' He stood again with a knowing look. 'Harmless old bugger.'

'But he doesn't own the land, does he? Can be moved on.' Long socks spoke confidently.

'Yeah. Wouldn't like it o'course. Likes his privacy.'

Red nose looked at large paunch and then at long socks. 'Guess the company'll have to find him another place.'

'Maybe. But they'd have to be real careful.'

'Oh, they would be. Could maybe give him a house some place. Better than that dump.'

Bert was fairly certain Jim wouldn't want to leave where he was. 'He built it, ya know. With his bare hands.'

Red nose smirked. 'Not much of a builder, I'd say. Wouldn't win the award for the house of the year.'

'Still, it's his home. Gotta respect that.' Bert felt antipathy stretch across the bar.

One of them muttered something that sounded like 'We'll see', as the three of them took their beers and went to stand near the door.

Their murmurings were not loud enough for Bert to hear.

After a few minutes, they stood their empty glasses on the nearby shelf and one of them touched his forehead in acknowledgment. 'See ya tomorrow,' he said before they went outside.

Bert couldn't leave the pub. Locals would be coming in soon. But Madge saw the men leave. The Land Rover went under the railway bridge and disappeared as she walked to the pub.

'What you learn, Bert? Anythin' intrestin'?'

'They work for some American company. They was talkin' about minerals. Apparently, they think Sandhill got plenty. Loads of minerals in the sand there. Wanna take some rooms here next week. Just fer a while, they said.'

'I've heard of mineral sands,' Madge said. 'Didn't know they were on Sandhill but.'

Bert thought for a moment, stared out toward the sea. 'Reckon where there's sand, there's likely ter be minerals.' He spoke slowly as though testing the idea.

'Spose.' Madge wasn't sure what it all meant. Was disappointed by this seemingly unexciting news.

'One of em said Jim'll have ter go. Asked me if the caravan park is okay.'

'Jim in a caravan! Why? He's doin' no harm where he is.' She was shocked.

'Said they'd find him somewhere else ter live,' Bert hastened to add. He chuckled. 'Said his place wouldn't win no awards.'

'No,' Madge was puffed out like an angry pigeon. 'But it's his home. He's not doin' anybody no harm.'

'Might be in the way,' Bert ventured. He could see this idea of moving Jim was going over like a lead balloon. 'Here, have one on me, Madge.' He pulled a glass from the rack, grinned at her.

'Too early in the day fer me,' Madge said. 'I haven't shut up shop.' She moved to the door and turned. 'He's well known. Jim. Reckon there'll be more than just me as gets angry if he's shifted.' She gave Bert a warning look.

'Don't blame me,' he said. 'I didn't say he had ter go.'

But Madge had stumped out and he watched her large frame walk purposely back to her store. He sighed. It seemed to him at that moment as though the three men were harbingers of news they could all well do without.

<h1 style="text-align:center">13</h1>

Jim rose early. 'Up with the birds,' he used to say, or 'Up at sparrow's fart.'

Showering was an intermittent affair and dependent on the weather. An outside system, his shower consisted of a small stone slab with a hose slung above, which was attached to the water tank. Frogs loved it and birds would sometimes splash in the water left behind in a dent in the slab.

A battered coffee pot would produce Jim's first drink of the day when the light was still the pale yellow of dawn. He slurped it down, lit up a cigarette and breathed out a sigh of contentment. He'd thought about the heath and the sand last night, had slept with it tugging at him. Space. A change from the rainforest. Bloody magnificent open space. That was what called to him.

He grabbed his old straw hat, the easel, slung his backpack on one shoulder and made for outside. He'd be gone for a few hours. Reminded himself to take water so filled an empty bottle from the tank. He tapped the side of the tank several times. Sounded pretty full. Goodo!

Birds' cries had taken over from the shrieks of flying foxes that had already hung themselves to sleep, black rags in the taller trees. There was the sweet perfume of a camphor laurel. Dense shrubs reached across the track, ferns and elkhorns sprayed out from trees further back. At certain times of the year, orchids flashed their miniature, exotic brilliance. Few visitors knew where to look for them. Jim saw it as all part of his world, his garden of Eden.

The path wove its way for a good five minutes. His bare feet made marks in the sandy soil. Then it suddenly opened up. Like the sack at his door. Wallum scrub with huge dunes beyond. A stage backdrop, set in open sea.

He walked further towards that great expanse of blue then set down his backpack, opened his easel, the four legs digging deep into the sand. He was forced to kneel. Screeching seabirds wheeled above and around him. In the distance was the roar of the waves mixed with the breeze that sang of salt and sea.

For an hour or more, he was absorbed in his interpretation of the immediate world. Nothing else mattered. Time was irrelevant.

It was his knees that finally forced him to stop, stand and stretch. He reached for his tobacco pouch and papers. Rolled a cigarette and crouched with his back to the wind to light it. Time to go back.

He walked slowly now. Exhausted as he always was from these days of intense concentration.

When he came closer to his shack, his eyes focused on a huge boat. More like a ship. Men moving about. A ramp had been let down to the little beach and something that looked like a privy was being pushed down it. This couldn't surely be happening. Not on this island. He dropped his easel and bag of materials. Walked towards the boat.

One of the men saw him. 'Hi!' He was a big man with a paunch. Not one of the men he'd seen before. This one looked more like a worker. Would be scary in a fight.

'Hi!' Jim responded. 'What's all this for?' No room for politeness.

'Setting up fer sand mining.'

The other men were still working to gradually slide the privy up the beach.

'Gotta bring in a dredger next ter dig out the sand, mate. Somehow get em all across the island to where it's all gunna happen.'

'So you're saying you're mining the sand for minerals?'

'That's right, mate. On the other side. Surfing beach. Not here.'

It was tempting to say he was not a mate but Jim knew he was no Goliath. Not even David.

'What's the company?'

'MinWorx. Spelt with an x. Biggest in the business.'

Helpless fury was making Jim shake. He balled his fists. Took a deep breath. 'Got government approval of course?'

'You betcha. What's it to you, anyway?'

'I live here, that's all.'

'Where's your house?'

'Over there.' Jim flapped a hand.

'Kinda camping then?'

'No. I live here permanently.'

'Ah well…you'll be right. We're working the other side.' The man grinned, tipped his cap. Turned back to see what the others were doing.

Jim knew his anger was wasted. He went inside. Sat and watched until the men returned to their boat, pulled up the ramp and motored off.

Such a sense of impotence was new to him. He was a weak shit. Should have let them have it. But it wasn't them. It came from some unseen powerful force he couldn't communicate with. Theirs was a different language.

His thoughts were jumbled. Recriminations, anger, frustration. He lay on his bed and stared at the ceiling. The flaking paint mixed with rust from the iron roof strangely calmed him. Always did. Shapes appeared. Contorted faces, trees twisting up or spilling down towards him. This was what he knew. His world.

Finally, he got up and went out again to pull his tobacco and papers from his backpack. Nobody in town would want this. It wasn't about him. The island was a sanctuary for life. All life. Free to live as creatures and plants chose. This was worth fighting for, much as he hated fights. He needed time to sort out his thoughts. Think what to do next.

14

The mining men who moved in said there'd be more arriving but didn't say when.

Bert was glad of the extra money, but a growing sense of dislocation gnawed at his guts. The little town was being invaded. These men smelt of danger, something sinister. He couldn't put his finger on it. Thought he'd test Tracy. Young, but smart as fresh paint.

'Heard about the sand mining on Sandhill, Trace?'

'Heard today,' she said. 'Well, actually, I heard a kinda rumour a few days ago.'

'Think it's a good idea?'

'Nah. Don't think it'll do much for Sandhill. Not in the end.' She wiped an ashtray on the bar as she spoke. 'Reckon it's some big business bloke who wants to make money, doesn't care about the place.' Then she added, 'Or us.'

'But you don't know they'll do damage. Might be just a bit of sand sucked up. The minerals taken out. Sand put back again. Just as it was.'

Tracy shook her head. 'Nah, betcha it won't be the same. Reckon Sandhill's good the way it is. This town's good the way it is. Boring as all get out,' she grinned at Bert, 'but kinda predictable. Peaceful sort of.' She moved towards the tables, rag in hand. 'And anyway,' she flashed him a look over her shoulder, 'I'll bet they won't give a damn about us in the end.'

A couple of guys from the timber yard came in late in the afternoon for a pint. 'Sand mine on the island, good news, bring money into the town. Lotsa jobs.'

'And where will the people wanting them jobs come from?'

'Men like us.' The two timber men exchanged looks. 'Not so much work in timber lately. We've had to cut back.'

Bert struggled to express what he felt about that. Tracy's last words hung over the bar. Echoed all day. Along with the swish of the ceiling fans.'

At the hostel, Steve found he was no longer alone in the dormitory. Three men had moved in while he was at work. Big blokes, they had the contents of duffle bags strewn about the room. One man with red hair and another guy going grey were bent over their bags. A third was standing looking out the high window.

The redhead turned to look up at Steve. 'Me name's Blue,' he said. 'You on the bottom bunk?'

'Yes. I'm Steve. Is that okay?' Steve had a feeling it wasn't.

'Reckon you could go up. You're young.' The tone of voice suggested Steve shouldn't argue.

The grey-haired bloke looked up, then stood and Steve was conscious of how big he was. He stared down at Steve. 'What you doin' here, son? This gotta be the arse end of the fuckin' town.'

'I work at the newsagency.' These weren't going to be good room mates.

'Newsagency, hey?' He gave a brief laugh. 'Looks like he should still be at school. Don't ya reckon, Blue?'

Blue had stood now and the two of them looked Steve up and down. Steve felt suddenly overpowered. As though he might suffocate. Why were these men here? Suddenly? Now?

'I'm Stan,' the grey head said. 'We're here ter do some real work, son. On Sandhill Island. Godforsaken little island in the middle of fucking nowhere. Set the place up fer sand mining.'

'On the island?' Steve struggled with the idea.

'That's what I said, son.' He turned away to speak to the bloke who was standing at the window. 'Come on, Murph. Let's go to the bloody pub. I need a beer.'

'Gotta make a pit stop,' the guy muttered, heading for the bathroom.

'Someone lives there,' Steve said, his voice sounding loud to his own ears. 'On the island.' He thought of Jim and how small he would look beside these giants.

There was silence for a second. The big men stared at Steve. 'That a fact, son?' The way that was said, it made Steve feel a child again. 'Well, I don't think you should worry your young head about it. The boss'll take care of him.'

What did that mean? Sounded ominous. Steve tried to remain calm. 'Are you working for a big company?'

'One of the biggest. MinWorx. You wouldn't have heard of it, son.'

Steve hadn't. 'So what do they do?'

'We told you.' Stan was obviously bored with the questions, 'We're organising the gear fer sand mining. Dredges and stuff. Takes a while to set up.'

Murph came out of the bathroom. 'I thought we was goin' to the pub.'

'Waiting for you, ya slack arse,' Blue said, before addressing Steve in a way that suggested there would be no further discussion. 'While we're gone, just shift your gear to the top, son.'

After they'd left, Steve absorbed the news. What did sand mining entail? Would Jim know about it already? He felt he needed to talk to Tracy but she wouldn't be at the pub now. Would've gone home. As he left the hostel, he saw Madge come out of her shop and begin to sweep out front.

'Did you know they're going to mine on Humpback?' he asked when he came level with her.

'Yes,' Madge stopped sweeping. Looked at Steve. 'What you heard?'

'Sand mining. Island's got lots of minerals, apparently. Men staying at the hostel told me.'

'Be the end of the place.' Madge sounded disgusted. 'Bloody wreck the joint.'

'I wonder if it'll affect Jim.'

'Course it will. But it's not just about him. It's more than that, I reckon.'

Steve thought of what little he'd seen. The trees round the shack. The shack itself. He'd not thought of it before. Probably what was called the natural environment. Was starting to become a topic in his geography class. Never thought about it until then. Not about what it really meant.

'You wanna go have a look sometime,' Madge was saying. 'Unspoilt it is…or was. Won't be unspoilt much longer but. Been like it is now fer…fer hundreds of years. Thousands prob'ly.' She was red in the face.

'I've only been to see the artist. Jim. His shack. Seemed a nice old guy.'

'He's okay. Lives in a mess o'course. Wouldn't hurt a fly but. Don't understand his paintings but they sell apparently. Always pays me for his groceries up front. Never owes me nothing.' She chuckled. 'See that dinghy comin' in from Sandhill and I know what's driving him. Tobacco and papers. Always rolls his own.'

'I know. I've seen him.'

'Well, next time ya go, have a look around the place a bit more. Real wild, it is. Trees and ferns. Animals and birds. Unspoilt.'

Steve promised himself he'd do that but for the moment he'd settle for a pie and tomato sauce.

'That your dinner?' Madge asked, her eyes on him.'

'Guess so.'

'Not good enough fer a young man like you.' Her button eyes probed. 'Your mum wouldn't approve, I'll bet. Where is your mum? Dead is she?' She waited but got no response. 'Or did ya have a falling out?'

'Mum's okay,' he said. I just wanted to see the world a bit.' He felt vulnerable under her gaze and added defiantly, 'She knows I'm here.'

'But she'd want you ter have more than pie 'n' sauce, I'll bet.'

'It's okay.' Steve mustered his dignity. Walked towards the door. 'See you,' he said.

Back at the hostel, the men were still not around. Steve climbed up to the top bunk and savoured his pie. No good thinking about the island or Jim tonight. Nothing he could do. Trace might know. But it was Saturday and she would have gone home now. Could maybe try to catch her tomorrow. But Sunday was a big day at the pub. Monday was her day off.

He finished his pie and lay on his back for a few minutes, thinking. He wasn't tired so got up again and, for want of somewhere to go, wandered down to the jetty. Boats bobbed but no signs of life. He walked then in the other direction, out of town under the railway bridge, following the road. Twilight came and went in a blink in this part of the world. Darkness was a thick curtain, heavy and hot. A truck grumbled past, lights blazing. Steve jumped sideways into the ditch. Remembered he was walking on the wrong side of the road so crossed over. Always walk facing the oncoming traffic.

It was flat here and distant lights twinkled. A farmhouse? Tracy's uncle's? Apart from that, the place seemed empty, almost drained of life out here. Kind of lonely. Out here, the noise of the cicadas seemed even louder. Other than cicadas, there were no more sounds to disturb the darkness. He could hear his own breath. His footsteps. As he strode out, each step gave him a real sense of freedom, a kind of exhilaration. He could do anything. Whatever the future threw at him. He clenched and unclenched his fists. Felt the muscles on his arms tense. This wasn't the most exciting place in the world but it was his new beginning. The world could be your oyster, son. He was sweating but even that made him feel confident. Male. Powerful.

A utility came behind him. Stopped.

'What the hell you doing out here?' a voice from the cabin asked.

'Just walking. Getting the lie of the land.'

'A bit hard in the dark, mate.'

Steve recognised the face. One of the guys he'd met at the pub that night.

'Steve, isn't it? C'mon. Hop in. I'm Rob. There's a snooker game at Davo's.'

Steve climbed in and noticed the familiar farmyard smell. There were bits of straw on the seat and on the floor.

'You shoulda given us a ring. Coulda picked you up. Where did you say you're hanging out?'

'At the hostel.'

'Okay, is it? Always looks a bit derelict. Backpackers stop there sometimes. When there's any work around.' He laughed. 'Work's a bit too hard for some of 'em, though. Fencing and stuff. Where you working?'

'Newsagency.'

'Ah. Joe's all right. You were lucky there.'

The ute stopped outside a brilliantly lit old house. Timber. High set. Wide veranda out front. There were cars and utes parked at various angles out the front. As soon as the engine died, the sounds of laughter and voices pierced the night. A couple of figures were silhouetted, dark shapes against the light.

They went up the front steps and round to the side veranda. Out the back, guys and girls were watching a game of snooker. Beer was in evidence. Cans and stubbies but nobody appeared any the worse for wear. Cigarette smoke spiralled outside as well as in. Someone offered Steve a Marlborough but he refused. Not something he'd ever seriously been interested in. Not since he'd smoked three cigarettes in a row and promptly thrown up.

'Want a beer?' a guy named Alex asked. He was the host apparently.

'Thanks.'

With glass in hand, Steve felt one of the group.

'Hi ya!'

He spun round and recognised Mel. 'Hi!' He grinned. 'Tracy here?'

'Nah. Her aunt doesn't let her out on Saturday nights too often. Thinks all men are out to take advantage of her.' Mel giggled. 'Dunno how she puts up with them. Nice enough but strict as all get out.'

The beer was relaxing and the friendly banter was what Steve had been missing.

'Wanna have a go?' A guy named Ace held out a cue.

'Okay.' He would normally have been shy of being watched by people he didn't know but the alcohol had blotted that out. He took the cue and watched as the balls were laid out on the cloth. There was a moment's silence as he lined up. Bent at the hips. Made a bridge with his finger and thumb.

His first shot was wide of the mark but on his next turn he shot the blue ball into a cushion. That broke the ice and the encouraging words mixed with jokes grew louder as he and Ace gradually potted the balls into the pockets.

The night wore on and Steve was unaware of the actual time. Then without an obvious signal, members of the group began moving towards the door and motors hummed in the yard.

'Want a lift home?' Rob, the guy who'd brought him, offered.

'That'd be great.'

'Surf, do you? 'Rob asked.

'Not very good but I like it. Used to do a bit in Sydney and down the South Coast when we went on holidays.'

'Some good beaches round here.' Rob glanced at him. 'Sandhill's the best. On the far side. Good waves there. I could pick you up. Tomorrow if you like.'

'That'd be great!'

Steve thought of Jim but only for a second. The artist could wait. He wasn't going away. The offer of surfing was more enticing. Meant he was part of this town's mob. Couldn't get much better than that. Sod bloody Sydney and university.

He and Rob chatted in monosyllables for the rest of the ride. Both of them suddenly tired.

Rob dropped him off outside the hostel. 'See you tomorrow. Seven. Right here,' he said, and waved as he drove off.

Steve felt exhausted but still glowed inside.

In the dormitory, the men were dark mounds on their bunks in the gloom. One of them was snoring. Steve undressed quickly and climbed silently into the upper bunk.

15

At seven on Sunday morning, as Steve pulled on his shorts, there came the sound of a car horn bleeping several times.

A mound in one of the bunks groaned. 'Jesus! That bugger should be shot.'

Steve picked up his thongs and left the dormitory as quietly as he could.

There was another guy already in Rob's truck and the tray was loaded with boards.

'Move over, Mac,' Rob said as Steve opened the cabin door.

'Hi.'

Steve felt callouses as Mac gripped his hand.

'Hear you're new in town. Managed a run-in with Andy. Not hard.'

'Got you a board in the back,' Rob said.

'Thanks. Haven't surfed for yonks.'

'I'm not much chop at it,' Mac proffered. 'You're not alone, mate.'

'It's just our fun. Away from the farm.' Rob grinned.

'D'you all farm?'

'Most of us. Dairy, pigs. One or two have bigger places. Grow avocados, macadamias.'

A new world for Steve. Tracy's olds had a dairy farm but she'd indicated she didn't like it. These guys seemed happily part of the farming community. Laid back.

As though aware of Steve's thoughts, Rob said, 'Good life on the land. Hard but.'

'Have to get up early?' Steve's measure of hard.

'Half-five in the winter, half-four in summer.' Mac spoke as though it was just something to put up with.

Steve reflected briefly that he'd never done that.

'The old man finds it difficult these days.' Mac went on. 'Mum's okay but Dad's ticker isn't what it was.'

'So what happens if he can't do it any more?' Steve noticed Rob's nails were bitten and his hands spoke of manual labour.

'I'll just have to take over completely, I guess.'

'All right for you,' Rob said. 'I've got a sister and a brother. Might be some problems when my father decides to quit.' He laughed. 'One of us will have to do something else. Dunno what I can do.'

'Your kid brother's smart, though, isn't he?'

'Rick's okay.' Rob glanced at Steve. 'He's only fourteen right now. Clever, Mum's told. You good at school?'

'Nah.' At least Steve could be honest on that one. 'I always make Dad mad as hell.'

The two blokes laughed in unison. Steve wasn't sure if they were laughing with him or at him.

They were at the wharf now.

'Well, let's see how you get on out there.' Rob leapt out and Steve slithered down.

Mac and Rob lifted out the boards.

'That one's for you,' Rob said.

There was a fairly old motorboat bobbing beside the wharf. Mac leapt onto the deck and Rob passed him the boards. Within minutes, they were motoring out to the island. Mac tossed the anchor over the side and, carrying their boards, they jumped into the waist-high water. It was cold at this hour, spraying up as they leapt so they were almost totally wet.

'Gotta carry the boards the rest of the way,' Rob said. 'It's not far.'

It seemed a long way to Steve as they walked in single file past Jim's place, where there was no sign of life. The track wound through the undergrowth and then through what seemed like jungle. Tall trees, vine encased, leaning together. Dim light. Heavy dampness. Then, after a while, they were out into the open. Low scrub in sandy soil. Even at this hour, it was warm underfoot. Rob led the way. Obviously knew this route well. None of them spoke.

At last, the beach spread out before them, the waves curled further out and created white froth on the sand. Amid the roar of the sea, soldier crabs scurried off, feeling the footsteps of man. It was all so untouched, wild and empty, smelling of salt sea air. Sea birds bobbed or wheeled overhead, strutted along the sand.

The three of them shed shirts and shorts before hefting their boards back on their shoulders and going down the sandy bank to the beach. The waves this morning, according to Mac, were not huge but large enough to be somewhat intimidating for Steve. He wished now that he'd made an effort to get to the beach more often.

Rob and Mac walked briskly ahead across the sand and into the water. Mac glanced back once. A challenge. Steve knew he had to measure up.

The sea sucked and rose up ahead but the three of them paddled out through the earlier waves, ducking the foam of breakers as they pushed on. Only after they had paddled beyond the last curling swell did they stop, sitting astride their boards, treading water, looking for the next promising ride. While they watched, Rob and Mac started to lie on their boards. Steve copied them, waiting for their next move. Rob was the first to go, closely followed by Mac. As the wave curled, they stood, knees bent, to ride with it towards the beach. Steve hesitated. Lost the moment. Had to wait for the next. It seemed an age and he tried to ignore the others. He had to prove himself. When the next big surge of a wave came, he went with it, obliterating his fear. As it broke, he tried to crouch on his board but felt himself thrown into the water and sucked under in the blue and white cascade. When he reached the shallows, he stood, choking and gasping for air. Rob and Mac were some distance away standing still to watch.

'You okay?' Rob shouted above the noise.

'Fine,' Steve shouted back, grinning as hard as he could. 'Be better next time.'

He turned and paddled out again. Knew the others were behind him. This time, he was the first to take the wave, ride with it, half stand and follow it in for a short while before he fell.

Again and again, he forced himself to paddle out beyond the breakers and watch for a big mound of blue he could ride. Again and again he fell, swallowed, gulped for air. He forgot about the other two…last night…Tracy. He was, he realised later, completely in the moment. Totally involved in pitting himself against the might of the sea.

Eventually, he saw the others were walking away, up the beach. They flopped down on the sand. He followed them, exhilarated but exhausted. His legs felt like lead.

'Given in at last?' Rob was grinning up at him.

'I guess.' Steve lay down beside the other two, the soft sand warm against his back.

Mac rolled onto his side and propped himself on one arm. 'You sure gave it a go,' he said.

Steve thought he detected admiration. Or was it his imagination?

'Soon make a champion.'

'Nah. Just wanted to ride one a while.' He wanted to be one of them but was so tired now he was afraid he'd never be able to stand up.

Then a bunch of guys came thumping down the bank onto the beach. Carrying boards. They acknowledged Rob and Mac. Gave a quizzical glance at Steve.

'You're a rowdy lot,' Mac said and laughed.

'You said it,' one of them answered. 'Didn't come here to be quiet.'

'Surf's good,' Mac said. 'Better than it looks.'

They watched as the newly arrived hoisted their boards and walked down to the water.

Rob stretched and stood up. 'C'mon,' he said, 'let's go back. Find a beer somewhere.'

Steve forced himself to stand, to walk back to the boat. Back in the ute again, he almost fell asleep and woke only as they arrived at the pub he'd not tried yet.

The bar was a noisy place, brimming with young people, girls out in the beer garden. It was clearly the chosen meeting place this weekend. An unspoken agreement made last night, perhaps?

Steve felt something akin to pride when a male voice called out, 'Hi, Steve.'

The beer was cold and he felt his youth slide away with each swallow.

16

Jim slung the rope into the tinnie and set off for the mainland. Sunday. Wasn't often he came to town at the weekend. Too many people about. He'd heard some youngsters pass by earlier. Going to the surfing beach, no doubt. Never bothered him. Now, as he rowed, he remembered that Madge was closed on Sundays. Still, he needed to find out what the hell was going on. If anyone knew, Bert at the pub might fill him in.

As he passed the newsagency, he noticed a large sign in the window. Stopped to read it.

MinWorx Co Pty Ltd
An information evening will be held in the
Sandpiper Bay Public School Hall
Sunday 5 December at 6 p.m.
Explaining to local residents MinWorx plans for sand mining
on Sandhill Island and to answer any queries they may have.

And there was a sort of map too, a diagram of squares on the island it looked like. Seemed to cover a lot of it.

Any bloody queries! He'd have a few.

At the pub, Bert was leaning forward over the counter, his favourite position. Looked glued to it. Too early for many to be around. A couple of old codgers perched on stools staring into their beers.

Jim wasn't known for aggression but now it was clear the old man looked ready for a fight. His voice was stronger than usual, his eyes held Bert's. 'What the hell is this mining lot doing?'

'Gunna make us all rich,' Bert chuckled in an effort to sound light-hearted. Calm the old fella down.

'Oh yeah! It'll destroy Sandhill, the natural beauty.' Not enough of an audience here, Jim thought. Better to save his breath. But before he left, he needed to see if he could stir some reaction. 'You seen the map? Shows you what they're planning.'

'I seen it,' one of the old blokes said. 'Not sure what it means but.'

'Me neither,' said the other.' Best go to the meeting to find out, I reckon.'

'You c'n bet your life I'll be there. How 'bout you, Bert?' Jim wanted to ascertain if the publican was seriously thinking about it.

'Reckon there's two sides to this argument, Jim.' Bert didn't want to antagonise the old bloke but he'd heard some of the mutterings of others. 'Could do a lot fer the town.'

A couple of younger blokes had come into the pub. They looked at Jim and then at each other. Winked.

But Jim was gathering momentum. 'You might think that, Bert, but it's not the reality of it. We'll all be worse off. This is a nice sleepy backwater. The way we've all lived since for…for…ever. Peaceful. Content. Letting everyone do what they do best. All that will change. You mark my words. It's not only the island. The town will change too. Not for the better either.'

One of the men standing near the bar gave a disparaging snort. 'Dunno why it won't be better for most. Jobs. Money in the place, and what about the tourists? Money'll make for more things. Like a swimming pool, tennis courts maybe. It'll be the place to come then.'

'Holidaymakers won't want to be around mining of any sort. And the miners will be here today, gone tomorrow. Think they're better than us. Make demands for things nobody's ever wanted before. Then, when we've all got used to them, they'll up and leave but they won't tidy up after themselves. Not bloody likely. The island will be ruined, the birds and animals gone.'

Another man laughed. 'Wouldn't mind if the snakes were gone.'

Several others chuckled.

'You mark my words,' Jim went on. 'We'll discover we've not made all that promised money. There still won't be a permanent doctor, a soccer field or those things we've always wanted. Just destruction of the very things we all love. That's what it'll do for this town.' He paused to gather momentum. 'They'll ride roughshod all over us, demand what they want, then leave us with bloody nothing. All so a mining company can get rich. Greedy uncaring bastards.' He turned to Bert. Fixed his eyes on the publican. 'That's what it's all about, Bert. Greed.'

In the middle of his tirade, Tracy appeared from out the back veranda, broom in hand. The men at the bar muttered, shifted their boots, avoided eye contact.

'You're right, Jim,' she said, smiling at him. 'But at the meeting I reckon more people will be for it than against it.'

She had seen the sign the day before. Had raised it with her uncle and aunt. They seemed to think it a great idea. But then they never went to Sandhill. Didn't really care a jot for the natural world. That, for them, meant cows in the paddock. A livelihood. The only one they knew. Animals didn't mean much other than a source of income. Every so often when a cow got a bit old for breeding and milking, they'd take it to the nearby abattoir. They'd have beef for weeks then. Perhaps some farmers did care but she only knew the farm she lived on. Even in her teens, Tracy had come to the conclusion that cows were living creatures. Not copies of her but with a language and lives of their own. She had sometimes looked into the soft brown eyes of a cow, wondering what they knew or understood.

When she'd spoken of such a thing with her uncle, he'd just laughed. 'They're animals, for God's sake, Trace.' And that had been the end of it.

'There's plants on that island, Tracy, that are so rare they make botanists go crazy with excitement.' Jim's words were aimed directly to her. As if he knew she'd understand.

Tracy didn't know much about plants but she respected Jim's knowledge. His talk of 'feeling' in art had caused her to think more about a lot of things. Even if he was weird, he had shown a kind of wisdom she'd not known before. He'd got on with Steve too. Where was Steve? Probably still in bed. He didn't work Sundays. Lucky bastard! Seemed she never stopped. The pub, the farm, the pub, the farm. Her life. She fought off the sense of frustration she often felt these days.

'Everyone should attend,' Jim was saying now to those who had gradually assembled in the bar.

She guessed everyone was bored by the old man jabbering on about the island, like he owned it. Well, he did, in a kind of way.

'We've gotta protect Sandhill, the plants…the creatures that live there.'

'Yeah, well…' Bert clearly wanted to forget it all. He pulled another beer and winked at the man he was serving.

'I guess we all got to go to the meeting anyway,' Jim said. 'You people need to have your say.' He surveyed the group but all eyes were lowered. 'Don't say I didn't warn you,' he said as he pushed open the door and left the pub.

There was silence for a couple of seconds. Then Bert spoke, 'Course he wants to keep the island to himself. Isn't thinking about other people, the jobs.' Tracy opened her mouth to argue but thought better of it. There was an atmosphere of antipathy. She realised she'd do no good.

Later, she saw Jim wandering towards the wharf again and thought how kind of shrunk he looked. An old man. But he was different. Special to her mind, and she wanted to run after him. Tell him she was behind him in his desire to protect the island but she knew she couldn't. There were still tables outside to wipe down.

At around five o'clock, blokes usually came into the pub for a beer to unwind. The place perked up a bit. But Tracy had to be home by five thirty, so she could never hear the gossip. She would have liked to hang around. Especially tonight. Hear what effect Jim's outburst had had. What the men thought about the mining. Reluctantly, she took off her apron and went to hang it up out back. When she returned on her way to get her bike, she saw Andy had taken up a position at the counter. He saw her come in, seemed to look her up and down as though measuring her. She tried to ignore him but sensed his eyes followed her as she crossed the room. What was it about him? Whatever it was, he gave her a kind of creepy feeling. As if she was a mouse being watched by an owl or, worse, an eagle. She pulled her bike out of the rack and pedalled home, trying to erase the image from her mind.

17

'Where the hell you been?' Tracy's eyes were glowing embers of anger. 'Shoulda been here when Jim came. He's really upset over the mining. You shoulda helped him tell people. I don't think the guys in the pub believed him cos he's old and…and different.'

Her anger was so directed at him that Steve initially froze but then his flight or fight response took hold. 'I have a life,' he said. 'Don't blame me for your…your own…inadequacy.' Lovely word that. Inadequacy. Sounded like one of his father's. 'You could have helped the old man. Why was it up to me?'

'I was working when he came in. I couldn't stand up to all those blokes. Not on my own.'

'And I could, I suppose?' Steve tried to ignore a sense of guilt. He'd totally forgotten Jim, the island and even Tracy.

'You coulda tried. Blokes listen to other blokes. Not to a woman. Not to me, anyway.'

'I try to listen to you,' Steve gave a wry smile. 'Reckon lots of people listen to you, Trace.

'Well, anyway…' The fury had gone out of her.

'So Jim went home?'

'Eventually. Tried to tell people to go to the meeting.' She wasn't going to tell Steve about Andy, her sense of helplessness.

'I think people will go anyway.'

'I dunno so much. They just don't get it. They think it's only Jim wanting to live on the island. Undisturbed.'

'I guess that's how they probably see it.'

'Oh jeez, why don't people realise it's about more than that? They don't seem to think about things. People are so…so…'

'Apathetic.'

'Apathetic.' The word tasted nice. 'Yeah.'

'Well, we aren't. We'll go to the meeting anyway.'

'Yeah, but what if nobody else comes? The mining lot will think they've got it all sewn up.'

'Well, we got to try to get as many people as possible to attend.'

'And how we gonna do that?'

Steve thought about how things had been done at school. The weekly bulletin. But he didn't know exactly how it had been done. A machine they referred to as 'the roneo machine' in a room the students weren't allowed to enter. Anyway, there was no access to one of those here.

'If we designed a kind of advert for it and made lots of copies, we could put them in people's letter boxes.'

Tracy gave a screech-like laugh, 'Lots of copies! Letter boxes! You gotta be joking!'

'I reckon there's a way. Got to be.' He looked at her seriously. 'What's wrong with letter boxes?'

'You got any idea of how far apart they are. Bloody miles.'

'So...?'

'Take us all day and we haven't got that much time. And anyway, how are you gonna make lots of copies?'

'Reckon Jim might know the answer to that.'

Tracy thought about that but looked dubious. 'I dunno.'

'We could go see him. Ask.'

'Too late now. It's nearly six o'clock and I oughta be home anyway.'

She turned and went to collect her bike from the rack. 'See ya,' she said with a wave.

Steve stood for a few moments. Saw her sit astride her bike before peddling off. He wondered what her uncle and aunt were like. They sounded mean. But maybe they just didn't try to understand. Like his parents. The thought of them made the old resentment bubble but he felt a bit guilty as well. Maybe most people felt like that about their parents. A mixture of emotions. Complicated. Maybe life wasn't as simple as he'd thought it was. The guys he'd met at the party, gone surfing with, had been friendly and he'd felt one of them. Even though they weren't the kind he'd have mixed with in Sydney. But those guys from school hadn't ever mixed with many others outside their own patch. Nice enough to others in a polite kind of way but you had to kind of belong. State school guys didn't cut it. Not really. The guys here didn't seem to care where he went to school. Or if he even went. Had he been a snob before? A snob. Him! He'd never thought he was. It was a word people used for the stuck up. He wasn't, was he? But maybe he was. Were his family? Still in thought, he wandered down to the jetty.

A couple of blokes were working on their inboard engine. Didn't look up. He stared down, working himself up to ask. But what was he doing? None of this was his worry. Still, Tracy had made him feel guilty. As though he was involved. Or should be.

'You guys going out this evening?' His voice wasn't his own. A bit squeaky, like he was still a kid. He cleared his throat. Tried again.

Both men glanced up.

'If we get this bloody thing started,' one of them said.

'C'n I get a lift to Sandhill? If you go out?'

'Spose. Could be a while, but. You in a hurry?'

'Nah. I c'n just hang around…if that's okay.'

The grunted response suggested he could do what he liked. Steve realised he was really tired and lent against a bollard, closing his eyes.

Who should one see to get help on this island mining thing? Must be someone. Someone with a bit of power. Then it came to him – a councillor! Maybe Jim knew one of them. He'd ask him. He stood again and looked down at the men on the boat. It was important to talk to Jim.

18

'Think his name's McKenny or McKinny…some name like that.' Jim stared into space, trying to remember. He went to the stove where the kettle was about to boil. 'Anyway, I can find out. Madge'll know… Let's have a good cuppa while you tell me why you want to know.'

'Not much to tell.' Steve felt deflated. 'I just thought someone should try to get a councillor on side.'

Why had he not thought of Madge? Jim was too old to remember things like names. Too old for much really. Poor bugger. For the first time, Steve felt a wave of pity for the artist mixed with anger and a kind of hopelessness. But why was he involved? Tracy's fault. It didn't seriously matter to Steve if they mined the island. They could wreck the place for all he cared. It was just an island. One of hundreds. It wasn't as though lots of people lived there. Only an old artist.

Jim put a mug down beside Steve where he sat staring out the door. He spoke gently. His old man's voice. 'You haven't seen this place, have you? Not really.'

'No. Only a bit. I came here with some guys to surf. Just wanted to get to the sea, I guess. Didn't notice much really.' He didn't add that he'd thought the place pretty boring, really. Nothing to do.

'When you've finished that, I'll take you for a bit of a walk. Show you why it's important to save it. Keep it the way it is.' He sipped noisily at his tea. 'Oh, I know you think it's just another island.' He gave Steve a sideways knowing look. 'But it's special. In my book, anyway. Sure, there are lots of islands, up and down the coast. They're all pretty unique in their own way but this one's extra special for me…and others who come here sometimes.' He chuckled. 'Like you came here to surf, but they know how special it is. Plants here nobody's even named. Birds that are rare on the mainland. They know they're safe here.'

'Animals here too? Are they special?' Steve knew he sounded as if he was mocking the old man and in a way he was.

'Thousands of flying foxes, brushtail possums and the odd ringtail. Lots of gliders. A few roos, of course, and wallabies. Some of the flying foxes are pretty rare.'

'Dingoes?'

'Yes. A few. They come around here sometimes but mostly I hear them far off at night. Keep themselves to themselves. True dingoes, not the crossbreeds that are usually around places like this.'

Steve had never had much interest in wild animals, never had any reason to be interested. Now he began to feel intrigued at the idea of dingoes running wild. 'Snakes, I'll bet?' he asked.

'A good few. Not interested in people, though. Just want to be left alone.' Jim chuckled again, 'Like me.' He grabbed a large torch from a shelf above his bed. 'Come on. Let's go have a gander.'

It was night now but the moon had taken up residence so there was a ghostly light illuminating the immediate area around the shack.

Jim's torch shone along the dirt path and Steve followed him.

'You must have seen rainforest,' Jim said, 'walked through it probably, haven't you?' He stood still. 'Listen!'

Steve had never before noticed the sounds of the night as he did at that moment. The crickets had died down but other noises, such as rustles, squeaks, flaps and scratches, had taken over. As they went further into the dense overgrowth, he was sure he saw small eyes among the leaves.

'Flying foxes,' Jim said. 'Only come out at night. Leave the island in search of food but they find some berries here. Nothing would grow without them. Them and the wild bees. They do the pollinating of the seeds the bats and birds drop. The fruit or flowers that come from the seeds. Endless cycle of life really. It's our job to leave them alone, let them get on with it.'

The air was heavy with the heat and a sweet scent mixed with the smell of decaying vegetation. It combined to create an exotic richness.

It was altogether another world for the younger man. The two walked silently along the path, Steve conscious of his own breath, following Jim. The tall trees were acting as sentinels, benignly watching their moves.

Quite suddenly, Jim stood still and angled the light from his torch. A wallaby, caught in the light, stood frozen for a moment then, when the beam of light fell away, hopped off into the night.

The stars seemed brighter than Steve had ever noticed them before. He stared up. They reminded him of the sparkles of fireworks. If he had been asked, he would have wanted to say it was all magic but he wasn't asked and anyway he felt almost embarrassed by the passing thought. A sudden image of his mates on the train station made him want to laugh at what they would see as stupidity but that thought was as quickly overtaken by his awareness of being free of them. Able to see things differently. Not needing to conform.

'You can hear the sea from here.'

There was the gentle swoosh of what must be waves. Everything was different at night. The sounds. The air was full of scents he couldn't name.

Jim shone the light on a nearby bush. 'Banksia,' he said. 'Pale yellow flowers. Die off pretty quickly. Go brown. Birds feed on the seeds. Marvellous cycle of life. You city fellas wouldn't see much like this, would you?'

'Is it true that the native plants need fire to release their seeds?'

'Sure is. But not in the rainforest at all. Too humid there to allow a fire for long.'

Steve stood absorbing as much as he could of the scene around him.

But then the old man turned. 'Best get back,' he said.

They pounded down the track, Steve following.

Then Jim stood still. He turned to look at Steve. 'Bit late for you to get back tonight. Got a spare mattress. Jim's eyes were gentle, his smile hesitant. 'If you like, that is.'

Steve could tell the old man was genuine, was allowing his usual privacy to be invaded. 'I gotta be at Joe's,' he said.

'I c'n take you back in the tinnie. Need some stuff at Madge's, any-way.'

'Thanks. That'd be great.'

Baked beans on toast had never tasted so good and the lumpy mattress seemed to embrace his exhaustion. He was asleep before Jim had blown out the lamp. Waking once in the night, he lay for a few moments, savouring being at one with nature. He felt sure his view of the world would never be quite the same again.

Early morning light filtered into the shack, a beam of sunlight slanting directly onto Steve's bed. He stretched and yawned before opening his eyes. Swivelling to look at Jim's bed, he realised the old man was already up. Looked at his watch. Seven o'clock. He hadn't slept like that for ages. There was a strong smell of coffee.

Jim came to stand by Steve's bed, holding out a mug. 'My brew might be a bit strong for you.'

Steve didn't like to say he wasn't a coffee drinker so he thanked the artist and sipped. A strong and bitter taste.

'Put hairs on your chest,' Jim said. 'What time you got to be at work?'

'Joe likes me there by ten thirty these days. He goes off for a break about then.'

'No problem. Get you there in plenty of time. I'd offer you breakfast but no bread at the moment. Have to call in at Madge's and get some more.'

The birds were creating their cacophony chorus so the world outside was absorbed into the room.

'Just like to show you a bit,' Jim said.

Steve wondered what he meant but then saw the artist had pulled out the drawing from his first visit. He was surprised that Jim still had it. He got up and dragged on his jeans, before going to where Jim stood staring at the black scribbles that were Steve's attempt to capture Tracy.

'Portraits are about more than features. Or should be. They're es-

sential o'course but it's the character of the sitter you got to try to capture.' He eyed Steve. 'That's the tricky bit. Discovering what the person
is like first up,' he laughed. 'Talk to em a bit while you study them.
Then it's bringing that out in the work. Not easy.'

Steve felt he'd never manage that. 'I don't think I'd be able to do
that,' he said.

'Course you can.' Jim was still studying the drawing. 'If you think
about it, her eyes are the thing. Paint would do it. Oils. Much harder
with a drawing. Come over another day and I'll show you what I mean.'

'I'd like that.' Steve was excited that the old man was prepared to
teach him. 'Kind of you…to give up time for me.' He felt chuffed and
more than a little surprised that he'd gained at least the interest of the
artist.

'Any day when you can get across.' Jim put down the drawing and
picked up Steve's mug from where he'd put it down. 'Right now, I'll
just stick this in the sink. Then we might as well be off.' He was moving
about the room as he spoke. 'Got a lot to do in the next few days.
Reckon we'd better find the name of one of those councillor blokes and
we'll go to see him. Tell him what's what.'

Steve had the niggling feeling that he was being swept up into something he'd had no plans for. Then an inner voice said, 'But that's life,
man. You stuck your neck out, so now you'll have to cop it.'

19

A visit to one of the local councillors, whose name they discovered was Reg Mossop, proved frustrating.

'Well, Mr…er…what did you say your name was?

'Jim Masters.'

'Oh, pleased to meet you, Mr Masters. Now what can I do to help?'

'We're concerned at the idea of sand mining on Humpback,' Jim sat forward on the chair in the councillor's office. 'We wondered what you think about it. We felt sure you'd be worried by what it may do to the island, the future of tourism in the area.'

'There's a meeting on Sunday at the local school hall and we were wondering if you're going. If you can help us,' Steve said, his eyes on the councillor.

Councillor Mossop deliberately looked blank. He knew about the meeting. Had been directly invited by one of the reps from the mining company – over a lunch that had lasted into late afternoon. 'Help you do what exactly?'

'We'd like to think someone official would be at the meeting on Sunday. Would present the facts of the case.'

'What facts?'

'The fact that the island is a pristine place. Rainforest in places and wallum scrub in others. Bloody vast areas of sand and fantastic bird life…'

'As well as all kinds of animals and reptiles.' Steve could see Councillor Mossop wasn't listening.

The councillor's eyes were glazed. 'I did go there once or twice when I was a kid, he said. Then he smiled in a polite, bored way. 'Good fishing. Not much else, though. No ice creams, I remember.' He laughed.

'Spose your council area is pretty large, so one small island doesn't mean much.' Jim sounded scathing.

Councillor Mossop bridled. 'Everywhere we represent is important, Mr Masters. I care. I most certainly do. I wouldn't be giving up my time if I didn't. I just have to think of the good of our community. What's good for them is good for all, I say.' He beamed.

'Well, this planned mining won't be good for the community,' Jim showed his anger. 'It'll be too late to protect the next generation's birthright if we don't act now. And you're supposed to represent the community – look after the land we live in.'

Councillor Mossop glowered. Who did this dishevelled little man think he was talking to? A councillor was elected by the majority of the people to represent them. For a second, the two men glared at each other.

Then the councillor sighed and gave a tight little smile. 'I think you're taking this problem to the wrong quarter. This isn't really a council matter. Much too big for us to handle.' He twirled his pencil. 'You know, you really need to talk to the local state member. He's the one who deals with such things.' He gave a chuckle at this and stood to hold out a hand. 'Sorry about that. Love to help but not our decision.'

Jim and Steve got the message and stood together. Jim turned for the door, ignoring the outstretched hand but Steve shook it. Noticed it was limp and a bit damp.

Out in the street, Jim snorted. 'He's supposed to represent us.'

Steve was trying to think and now spoke almost to himself. 'He said we should talk to the state member, whoever that is. I guess we should.'

'Hmm!' Jim snorted. 'Cup a coffee first wouldn't go amiss.'

20

The Honourable Michael Stuart, Member of the Legislative Assembly of New South Wales, was supposedly studying a submission for a mining lease. But he was, in fact, quietly perving on Samantha, his secretary, as she worked in her corner of the office. There was a glass wall between him and her so he could see her every move. When she bent forward to put a stack of paper into the printer, her cleavage made him shudder with excitement. These rare moments were secret thrills that made his office day. Familiarity with his wife of thirty-five years had caused that sexual titillation to vanish. Samantha looked up then and smiled. Not at her boss but at someone coming in the door that was outside his line of vision.

That tramp-like artist fellow he'd noticed around a few times and a young man he'd not seen before were in front of Samantha's desk. He picked up his phone and pretended to be in conversation.

Samantha looked in his direction and he heard her say, 'He's on the phone right now but I'll go in when he hangs up.'

The bulge in his trousers subsided. Shit! He'd have to deal with this.

'Mr Stuart, there are two gentlemen here to see you. I said I'd see if you have a few minutes.'

'Goodbye then, mate.' Mick put the headset back on the cradle. 'A few minutes, Samantha. I have to go out shortly.'

Jim and Steve stood in front of his desk. He'd have to ask them to sit. Too confrontational to leave them standing. Lowering over him.

'Yes?' he asked. 'Please do sit down.'

Jim and Steve took the two chairs opposite and the old man coughed before he spoke. The member of parliament thought he had a gentle but surprisingly authoritative voice. 'We're hoping you can be of some help…in your capacity as the local member.'

'Yes?'

'There's a mine been planned on Sandhill Island.'

'Yes, I know. It's been well advertised.'

Jim and Steve exchanged glances.

'There's a meeting to be held by the company, MinWorx on Sunday at the Sandpiper Bay School and we hoped you'd see our side of the story and could explain it to the mining crowd. And the locals. They don't understand what it could do to them. What it will mean.'

MLA Stuart had already been briefed by MinWorx to expect some backlash. But a youth and an old man. Really!

'Mr…er…?

'Jim. Jim Masters and this is Steve Hastings.'

'Well, Jim and Steve, I'll tell you what it will mean. It will mean jobs and real money for the town of Sandpiper Bay.'

'But it will also mean the loss of habitat for the native flora and fauna. It will mean the end of the life cycle that's been going on for thousands of years on the island.'

'Miners always leave things as they were.' Mick was used to speaking calmly and patiently. 'Let me assure you, we put stringent controls on them. They have to leave it so it can all gradually return to the way it was.'

'But it won't. Can't. It takes years and years for the vegetation to re-cover and by then the native animals and birds will be gone.'

'They'll come back.'

'No. They'll have died by the time it's a fit place for them to live in again. The animals can't all swim to the mainland and the birds can't set up new breeding grounds.'

Mick Stuart fidgeted with a pen. Why did these men make him feel uncomfortable? 'I think, perhaps you need to talk with your local coun-cillor. He's the more appropriate person to respond to your thoughts.'

'Oh, we have already,' Steve was surprised at the sound of his own voice. But now he had started, he had to go on. 'We plan to talk with anyone who's prepared to listen. We have to. It's not about us or even the people who are supposed to get jobs. It's about the future of the town, the whole area. Tourists won't come if there isn't good surfing and…and…' He ran out of words.

Mick Stuart was staring at Steve. Young whippersnapper, knew more than was good for him. New to the town, obviously. How dare he tell his older and better what to do. A troublemaker. Still, he mustn't lose his cool. Word would get out.

'Well, young man,' Mick smiled indulgently,' I suggest you continue to seek support from all quarters.' He stood up. 'I have to go out now.' He smiled again. 'No doubt I shall see you at the meeting on Sunday.'

When they got outside, Jim gave one of his frustrated snorts. 'Bloody useless idiots. How they ever get to be elected I've no idea.' Then he answered himself. 'Course, nobody is really interested. Happy for somebody else to do the job. Apathy. The curse of society.'

'So what do we do now?' Steve had run out of ideas.

'We talk to people and we go to the meeting, that's what we do.' Jim sounded determined. 'And at the meeting, we'll find out what's going on and how many people are agin it.' He looked at Steve. 'And we stir. That's what we do, Steve. We stir the possum, mate.'

21

Steve's weekends were often spent on the island. Jim had allowed him to use his oil paints and would often take him out to draw trees, scrub, bushes. Then they would retire to the shack, where his sketches became exciting experiments with paint oozing from tubes. Some Sundays were devoted to surfing.

Weeknights were often occupied with meeting up with his new-found mates. Sex, sport and booze were their frequent topics. Farming was a constant.

'Sorghum crop not so good this year. Reckon we'll have to back up the cattle fodder with something. Expensive but.'

'Should have dug silage trenches, mate.'

The local girls were sometimes referred to as hot chicks, which Steve was used to, although he noticed these guys weren't into doobies like many of his Sydney schoolmates, who thought smoking dope was really cool. In some ways, these guys were quite square by city standards, he realised, but he admired them for their focus on their farming lives. It was one thing for a farmer to get a bit pissed but a bloke would be stepping over the line if he used other drugs. Steve was sure of that. Most of them had gone to the local high schools, one or two of them had boarded for a while at one of the country private schools. They were church schools, some of them Catholic boys' colleges. He'd not been exposed to Catholics much. His mother had almost whispered the word, in the same way she mentioned divorce. Such differences were unacceptable in her world, or at least unmentionable. He'd not given it much thought before but now he sometimes felt his previously accepted standards had been turned on their heads.

On one occasion, the local priest had come into the pub.

'Hi, Father,' Rob said. 'How're you going?'

'Fine,' the priest had answered. He'd ordered a beer and when it arrived had drunk half his glass in quick time before pausing to wipe his upper lip with the back of his hand and grin at Rob. 'No sign of you at Confession of late.' An Irish accent made the man seem further removed from the local scene. But here he was. Accepted. Part of the community.

Steve tried to remember if he'd ever seen his local minister at any of the Sydney gatherings he'd attended. Not that his family went to church except at Christmas or weddings. He was pretty sure the few Catholics he knew went to church. Probably went to that thing they called Confession, he realised now. He'd always felt they belonged to a separate kind of club. Went to different schools, had different rules, stuck close together.

'Might see me there next week, Father,' Rob said and then laughed. 'Cows don't give me permission to get away till mid-morning, though.'

It all seemed so easy. So relaxed.

On several occasions after, Steve saw Father O'Brien, always identifiable as a priest by his black clothes and white collar, attending social gatherings. At a twenty-first birthday do, at a charity football match. The first time Steve and the priest exchanged a nod was, for Steve, a moment worthy of celebration. As though he'd crossed a narrow connecting bridge. He wondered sometimes about the priest's sex life and if he wanked off as other men did? Or did he maybe have a woman on the side?

One or two of his new mates had steady girlfriends. Mac was sometimes in the company of a really hot-looking chick. He'd introduced her as Loren and while she looked Steve up and down, she was clearly only interested in Mac. She came to the local football matches but appeared to be only around when Mac wanted her to be. Otherwise, he was his own man. There was so much that was different here from what Steve had always known, had accepted as being the way of things.

Now he'd ceased to feel quite so out of place in the country town, he began to notice different aspects of it, some likeable, others less so.

These guys seemed to have no desire to live differently from their parents or grandparents, were happy to remain farmers. 'Gotta live on the land,' they would have said. 'Only way to go.'

But had Steve thought of living differently before? He'd railed against his parents often enough. That had seemed the way of his peers and it was accepted in its own way that 'the olds' were out of touch. His sudden decision that he'd had enough had been the turning point and lately, occasionally, he'd felt more than a little pride mixed with surprise at his actions.

He wondered if Tracy was a Catholic. Did she expect to go on living in the area? Or did she feel like breaking out? What would she do differently if she had the chance? Probably nothing. Still, she apparently admired Jim for his difference and worldliness. But Jim was in a category of his own. Was impervious to rejections or ridicule by others.

Oh, shit! He owed the old man so much. Was learning from him in more ways than just art. He'd more or less promised Jim to help with his plans to get rid of the miners. He knew he didn't have to but he'd felt he should. It occurred to him suddenly that he was as trapped here as he'd been in Sydney. But this time it was different: it was his choice. For the moment. Anyway, walking away would be easier. Surely. But he already knew it wouldn't be.

<h1 style="text-align:center">22</h1>

Jim put on an unpatched pair of trousers for the meeting. Found an old pyjama cord to keep them up. Slicked back his grey hair and snipped off the ends of his beard. He looked okay.

The oars sliced the water as he rowed across to the mainland. It was low tide. He tied the boat to the first bollard and climbed the ladder. The place seemed deserted, apart from some people on the camping ground. He could vaguely hear what sounded like 'rhubarb, rhubarb' coming from the school hall. Mutterings bubbled into the evening sky.

As he rounded the corner towards the school, a few words rose above the rest. 'Not for us', 'about time', 'jobs'… He straightened his back. If this was going to mean a fight, he was up for it.

Closer still, he saw Madge. Huge, in a floral dress that made her look even larger. She reminded him of a giant mythical bird.

Out of nowhere, Joe appeared with Steve in tow. The door to the hall was opened and the crowd began moving inside.

Jim followed the stragglers. Took a seat near the back. Didn't recognise any of the others who shuffled into his row. Voices were magnified inside the hall.

A table had been set up out front on the stage. Glasses and a jug of water. A microphone sat on its stand. Steve must be up front. Probably with Joe. Jim couldn't see them.

Four men came up the steps onto the stage. Suits and ties. The chattering was lowered to mutterings or whispers. A few people tentatively clapped.

Three of the official-looking party sat behind the table.

One of them came to the mic. Tapped it. 'Can everybody hear me?' he asked.

There were grunts and 'yeah' from around Jim.

'So… Good evening. My name is Reg Brown and, as secretary of the northern arm of the company, I have been delegated to speak on behalf of MinWorx.' He cleared his throat, licked his lips and smiled. 'We believe you should know what has been planned for Sandhill Island.'

Expectant necks craned.

'At considerable expense to date, we have taken some samples and found the place is rich in minerals. As a result, a grid has been created and we're beginning to set up excavation machinery in preparation for mining. There are five areas that we foresee as being suitable, each one taking account of the terrain and the different machinery needed. There is a map to demonstrate the five areas, which will be available to see in the glass case outside the hall. We shall, of course, be requiring labour and I'm sure you will agree this will prove most beneficial to everyone in the town.'

There was a shuffle and muttering.

'And far beyond.'

Jim got to his feet. 'What I want to know is what you're going to do to rectify the damage…'

His voice was drowned by the amplified voice of Mr Brown. 'Damage, sir? There is virtually no damage caused by our kind of mining.'

'But if you dig up the sand, there's got to be damage to anything that lives in it.'

'Nothing much lives in sand Mr…er…Mr…'

There was some laughter.

'Masters. Jim Masters. There's a lot lives in the sand close to the beach. Plants. Banksias and other natives. Worms. Some of them rare.'

There was more laughter and a few muttered comments.

'I don't think a few worms will upset the balance of nature, Mr Masters.' Reg Brown laughed.

Steve turned to look directly at the artist standing at the back of the hall. Felt annoyance for the miners, mixed with embarrassment for Jim, who looked so small, his voice so 'old man'. The passion that exuded from him was obvious and unapologetic. When he'd turned, Steve also saw the three men who'd been sharing his room. They were sitting together and they reminded him of thugs he'd seen on TV. He took in Father O'Brien, standing near the door. Wondered if he was for or against.

Jim wasn't giving up. 'There's more than worms at stake and you men know it,'

Voices now broke out from among the audience. 'Oh, give over, old man'… 'Give the boss a chance'… 'You don't have a job to think of…'

One of the other men at the table stood and took over the mic. 'I think it only fair to say that you have a vested interest in Sandhill, Mr Masters. Am I not right?'

'It's a natural wonder. One of the marvels of this country.'

'And you live there.' There was triumph in the words. 'You, more than anyone, would be concerned to keep your island the way you like it. Never mind anybody else.'

'My home is only lent to me,' Jim said.

'Lent to you? By whom, Mr Masters?' Reg Brown had taken back the mic.

'The natural world. I live with nature, which allows me to stay because I do no harm to it. Your mining will harm nature.'

There was laughter, followed by whispers and murmurings from the crowd.

Then Madge was on her feet. Red and blue flowers spread their vibrancy about her large frame. 'Jim don't do any harm to nature. Like he said, he cares for it. I don't think you will. At least we should know what youse intend to do with the island when youse finish with it. Cos you will finish with it and we don't wanna see Sandhill finished too.'

She sat again with an emphatic plonk and there were a few claps and some 'good on you' noises.

'Madam, I can assure you we will leave the island just as we found it.' Mr Brown was conciliatory. 'But on the way, we'll be doing the town a favour by employing local labour and giving everyone some of the luxuries you've been previously denied. A football field, a clubhouse. Things you should have had years ago.'

At this point, the murmurs became audible. 'That's right…' 'About time we had some a them things…' 'Gotta move with the times…'

'What about the beach?' someone called out from the back. 'Our surf beach?'

'There's plenty of other beaches around,' Reg said firmly. 'I can't believe you only find good surf on Sandhill.'

'It's the best but.' The young man who had spoken subsided. Muttered.

Steve wanted to jump to Jim's defence but didn't know what to say. He sat on his hands and cursed himself. Joe was obviously not anxious to actively join the fray either. Mumbled to Steve every second or so.

Finally, he stood amid the angry rumblings around him. 'How long do you intend on remaining? I think we deserve some indication as to how long these jobs you talk about will be on offer.'

'Hard to say,' Reg said. 'But it would seem at this stage that we can look to working the area for a number of years.'

Voices generally sounded much more positive at this point. Steve noticed how a casual listener would have been able to discern the majority of sounds for and the fewer against without hearing any actual words.

Jim was on his feet again. 'And it won't take a number of years for the island to be ruined for ever.'

One of the young guys Steve had met at Rob's place was also on his feet. 'This is farming country round here. And we farmers are a conservative lot. We like the land as it is. It's been good to us and we want to keep it the way it's always been. Sounds to me like you're planning to change a lot of things. Maybe some of it for the better but an awful lot not. And we like our surfing beach the way it is.'

'I can assure you, sir. We shall do no harm to your farms. Mining isn't about that.'

'So what is it about?' another man shouted.

'It's about harvesting the bounty that nature has given us.'

'God spare us,' Joe muttered. 'Bounty that should be left where it is.'

The evening wore on with voices sometimes getting louder or aggressive and then quietening again.

'Well, we need some of the things you guys are offering. We'll be glad of the certainty of income with the jobs you promise. I'm all for the mine.' For this, one local man received a round of applause. 'Reality is we need money in the town. We've just been drifting along. Happily o'course. But we need a better future for our kids.'

The audience was divided. Voices rose up, for and against.

After minutes of shouts and more personal slanging matches, the meeting wound up. There was still excited discussion as people left the hall and drifted off into the night. The shadows of giant Moreton Bay fig trees and the fragrance of frangipani hung like a veil over the town.

As the audience disappeared, Steve saw Jim trudging down the road towards the jetty. He ran to catch up with the old man. Didn't know quite what to say but wanted to let Jim know he was impressed. 'You made them think a bit,' he said.

'Bloody fools.' Jim didn't slow down. Kept his eyes on the road ahead. 'It's not about me. Not the way they made it look.'

'I know.'

The old artist was shut off. Closed in his own world.

Steve walked with him towards the jetty but knew he wasn't making contact. 'See you,' he said.

Jim gave a grunt of acknowledgement but kept walking. Steve watched him for a moment. He tried to shrug off the whole affair but knew he couldn't.

Back at the hostel, the three men were muttering among themselves but became silent when Steve entered.

He undressed and went to climb up into the top bunk.

One of the men, Murph, stood in front of the ladder. 'Wouldn't like to think you're agin the mining.' His eyes were on Steve. 'Get it, son?'

Steve stared back. There were several seconds of silence before he said, 'I get it.' The moment of silent eyeballed defiance gave him a pleasing sense of power.

<h1 style="text-align:center">23</h1>

Tracy had just parked her bike. She was ready for work.

'You missed the meeting,' Steve said.

'I know.' She wasn't apologetic. 'I'm not encouraged to go into town on my own at night. 'And the olds weren't keen on going. Said they were too tired.'

'You oughta stand up to them.'

'Easy for you to say. They've been good to me.' She scuffed the ground with the toe of her right boot. Then she tossed back her hair and glared at Steve. 'Gonna take off soon, though. Go south. The big smoke.' She looked down again. 'You know what it's like down there. Big step for me but. They won't understand it.' She stared at him again. Accusingly. 'Once I go, I won't be able to change my mind.'

Steve felt sorry for her. Realised her vulnerability and felt protective. Male. He took her in his arms. She fitted so well. He didn't care if anyone was watching. Wanted this kiss to last. His tongue slithered over her lips. Prised them apart. Tasted her.

When he let her go, she grinned. Raised one eyebrow. 'You're older than you look.'

'What made you think I'm a kid?'

She shrugged. 'I dunno, really. Just when you said you were eighteen I thought you were lying.'

Steve grinned. 'I was then but not now.'

'Still too young for me anyway.' She flashed him a sideways grin. 'See ya.' She moved towards the pub.

He wanted to call after her but wasn't going to give her the satisfaction. He smiled to himself. Enjoyed a different sense of power even more than the feeling he'd had in the hostel. Wished he'd felt like that at the meeting. Remembering that was sobering.

He walked thoughtfully to the café. He'd get a cheese and ham roll for lunch. Inside, Madge was talking to a local man he'd seen around.

'On 2MC, it was. Nine o'clock. Or just after. I didn't think anyone like that'd be there, did you?'

'Nah.' The man was pocketing tobacco. 'Reckon it's interestin' to everyone but. Whose side were they on?'

'Neither, I s'pose. Well, they couldn't be really, could they? I mean… they had to kinda give both sides.'

The man nodded sagely. 'Only right. People'll make up their own minds.'

'Well,' Madge swelled, her pouter-pigeon look. 'I made up my mind. I can tell you that for nothing.' She became aware of Steve. 'And what c'n I do for you, young man?'

'Just a cheese and ham roll, please.'

Madge nodded in Steve's direction. 'Nice to hear a young person with good manners. 'Course you can. I'll make up a nice fresh roll for you right now.' She pulled a bread roll from the glass cabinet. Still speaking to the man at the counter. 'He's from down south. Working at Joe's. Aren't you, love?' She smiled. 'Hard work and good manners. Joe's a lucky man.'

'Yeah, well, I gotta get goin'.' The man moved towards the door. 'See ya, Madge.'

'See ya, Fitch.' She turned her button eyes on Steve. 'You hear it, did you?'

'What?'

'Course you couldn't. No TV or radio at the hostel, I'll bet.' She was buttering the roll. 'It was on 2MC. Nine o'clock.'

Steve was clearly baffled.

'Local radio station,' she explained. 'Talk on last night's meetin'. Recordin' of that minin' bloke tellin' his lies. People ringin' in.'

So word had got out. A radio station! Why hadn't he thought of that? Why hadn't anyone thought of it? Great publicity. Even if a good number of people were for it. Might make them think again. Would certainly make the people of Coffs aware of what was going on.

'And they were lies,' Madge was saying. 'Promising things. Like the politicians. Lotsa promises without really knowing how to bring them about. Here's your roll, son.' She passed the tissue-wrapped roll over the counter as Steve fished for the money. 'Sayin' they'll clean up. What a loada rubbish. Can't clean up after that kind of damage.'

Another bloke had come into the shop.

'Yes, Dan? Another sausage roll?' Without waiting for an answer, she went on, 'Downright desiccation of the environment, I call it.'

24

In the studio of radio station 2MC, the Mid-North Coast's favourite DJ, Jim Myles, pressed the play button on the cassette machine. The beat of music from Abba's song 'Dancing Queen' allowed him to sit back for a bit. He knew the song's duration by heart. Played it all the time. Listeners couldn't get enough.

Through the glass in the control room, Rachelle, the receptionist-cum-general factotum was reading something. She wasn't looking in his direction. Bugger, he thought. I could do with a cup of coffee. He tried waving his arms about a couple of times to no avail. The glass was thick and he didn't have time to go out and into the control room.

God, he was bored. Studies in journalism at university in Brisbane hadn't prepared him for this. He'd imagined a well-paid job at a Sydney radio or TV station. But such jobs were thin on the ground. Unless you knew someone or stood out from the crowd. He wasn't James Dean but he wasn't bad. He needed to lose some weight but sitting around in a studio all day did nothing for one's physique. Should go running or something but the thought of that always made him feel slightly sick. That kid, Beth, who hung around the studio a bit thought he was a spunk. Still, he hadn't made it big time, like one or two from his year. Maybe that was still to come. What he needed was a good story. One that would make the city stations sit up and take notice.

He sighed. Drummed his fingers on the desk. Time for another advert.

'And the time now is three forty-five. This is your old friend Mylesie, who's happy to be with you this glorious afternoon on the Mid-North Coast. Now, if you haven't yet visited Coff's Harbour's new pizza parlour, Crunchy Dream, then I suggest you hop down to Sandbar Street and order your evening meal. Take the drive and give Mum a well-earned rest tonight. Or better still, ring them on 6560 3242. Give them your address and order and they'll deliver your dinner in a box at the time you want it. Remember, 6560 3242. Say Mylesie sent you. You won't regret it. You just go down the road to Crunchy Dream. And now we have a song from…you guessed it…Elton John…'Goodbye Yellow Brick Road'.'

He sat back again and noticed Rachelle had vanished from the control room. At the same moment, she popped her head around the studio door and deposited a sheet of paper on his desk. More news of some kind.

'A report has just come in which may be of interest to you. It reads that the people of Sandpiper Bay are arguing over a sand-mining proposed for Sandhill Island. According to a local resident, a lease has been granted to an American-based company and mining is expected to begin within the next few weeks. Some of the locals are in favour of the jobs this will provide while others are opposed to it, wanting to maintain the island as it is. What do you think about this? We'd be interested in your views and, as usual, we can be contacted by phone on 6561 2838. Give us a call and let us know what you think.'

He doubted many would ring in. This island was just another island. He faded up the Elton John track.

The light on his phone flashed.

Rachelle, the receptionist's voice, sounded less bored than usual. 'There's a call from a lady called Tricia. Okay if I put her through?'

'Hello! Tricia, is it? Ringing about the island, are you?'

'I am, Mylesie. When I was a kid, we had camping holidays on Sandhill. Wonderful place. We used to go fishing and walk in the forest there. It taught me about the natural world, I can tell you. We swam heaps and we used to see whales out to sea. Enormous, they were. I reckon they wouldn't want to do anything to upset that place. Tourists go there a lot in the summer. Once they know about it o'course. Not flashy like some places. Just quiet and…and…natural, if you know what I mean.'

'Oh, indeed, I know what you mean, Tricia. Thank you for your call. Nice talking to you.'

His eyes were now on the track timing. Almost at the end of that song. He'd play the last track while he put more music in the other machine. He'd hardly thought it through when the phone was flashing again.

'This one's someone named Sheila. Seems okay.'

'I got three sons, Mylesie. They been lookin' for work for a long time. They can't afford to leave here and want to work locally. Hard to find anythin' round Sandpiper Bay. This mining company'll make it possible. Good for the town too.'

The next caller, a man, sounded irritated. 'Dunno what that lady is thinking, mate,' he said. It's not all about jobs. It's about tourism, fishing, surfing and camping. Not too many unspoilt places these days. I reckon those three boys need to learn to look after themselves. Go to the city and find a job there. Plenty of work if they go to look for it.'

Music might have to wait for a while. Mylesie was busy making what he was sure were the appropriate noises. The light hardly stopped flashing. Even Rachelle sounded awake.

Then a call came through from some mining bloke. Worked for a company called MinWorx. Wanted to talk about it on air. Explain how it would be good for the town. Okay by me, Mylesie thought. Just have to check it with the boss.

He'd never been to Sandpiper Bay. Too small for him. And he had no idea as to where this bloody island was. Just another island among hundreds along the coast. But maybe this one really was special. Seemed to create interest anyway. Maybe he should find out more. Might give him something to do on his next day off. He could go up to Sandpiper Bay and have a look.

At least this was going to be a busier afternoon.

25

Jim stared at the ceiling and contemplated his next move. Madge was on his side. Joe too. A good few others seemed to be. But there were an awful lot who weren't. He needed the support of the young guys. The farmers and the campers who used the island for surfing.

A lovely early morning yellow-blue sky but Jim wasn't feeling his best. His head ached and his guts felt delicate. Bloody old age! He poured a few drops of rum into his first coffee. That helped. He went outside. Stood still to sniff the air. Take stock.

The island always amazed him. Its rhythms. Now the veil of darkness had lifted, cockatoos screeched and circled. Lorikeets sent flashes of colour in low branches that bent under their weight. An ant hurried purposefully across one of his bare feet. The usual scurrying of life at the start of the day. Everything smelt clean, fresh. He felt an intruder. A somewhat dirty human, he thought, with a wry smile.

Inside again, he sat on the edge of his bed. Stared round the room. The beginnings of an idea niggled. His eyes lingered over a half-finished painting of the bush in rain. Quite liked that one. There were several other canvases stacked in one corner.

He needed to make people aware of what the island offered. The magic of the place. He got up to pull out the various paintings. Spread them around. He'd have to do a lot of work on some of them but it was feasible. The gallery guy in Sydney could wait.

He'd need to go and see where he could rent a place to hang his work. Now he had the paintings spread out, he had the urge to work on them but he must hold fire for a bit. Right now, he should go to talk to Bert and Joe. Or anyone who might be able to advise him on hanging space.

'I want to have an exhibition, Bert,' he said. 'Show people the island. How it is.'

'Tried the school? Would maybe let you have the hall.'

Jim considered it. Could ask anyway.

Later, he found this might be possible. Apparently, his name registered. An artist some already knew. Happened sometimes. But it always surprised him a bit.

Most importantly, there was a blank in the booking sheet against a Friday in three weeks' time.

He'd maybe manage it.

26

In the next month, it became hot and the caravan park became littered with tents and one or two kombi vans. Jeans and various articles of underwear hung from makeshift clothes lines and surfboards stood stacked like sentinels against the few trees that dotted the grounds.

When Steve went down to the jetty, he found a number of bare-topped blokes fishing over the side.

'Hi ya,' said one of them, a guy with long blond hair and a bit of a beard.

Steve grunted. He looked down at one of the few remaining boats. The others must have gone out early.

'You going over Sandhill way soon?' he called down.

An elderly bloke with a grey beard peered up at him. 'Not fer a while yet.'

That would doubtless be too late for Steve to get over and back before work. He sighed and turned to go.

'Unspoilt this,' the same fisherman said. 'The way we like it. And the surf's good. Some of us come every year around this time,' he indicated the camping ground with his head.

Steve reckoned the guy was trying to be friendly. A bit scruffy. Not the sort his mum would've wanted him to be around. He was inwardly grinning at the thought.

When Steve returned to the hostel that evening, his backpack was out near the manager's office. A few clothes spilled out.

'Why's that there?' he asked the manager.

The bloke had a sheepish expression. Couldn't look Steve in the eye. 'The fellas said they wanted the room to themselves.'

'And where am I supposed to go?'

'Dunno. But you can't stay here. They reckon you're trouble.' He turned away to go back into his office. 'With a capital T, son.'

Steve stuffed the spilling clothes into the backpack. Slung it onto one shoulder. 'If they want trouble, I'll show them what that is.'

He stepped out. Felt a sense of impotence mixed with rage like he'd felt with his father. He'd not felt anger much here before that. Now he realised it wasn't a good feeling. He saw red. That expression cut it. He wondered if he looked red. Certainly felt hot. Began somewhere in his guts. Felt he might choke with it.

At the pub, he downed a beer without tasting it. The place was crawling with men involved with the mine. He became conscious that eyes were on him. He ordered a second glass and remained at the bar, staring deliberately at one or two between sips. He knew his hands were shaking but hoped he'd hidden it. One man he eyeballed turned to his drinking mate, said something and they both laughed. The bastards! He'd show them.

Eventually, in as leisurely a fashion as he could muster, he slung his backpack over one shoulder again, headed out and walked towards the wharf. His fury was tempered by the thought that he had nowhere to go for the night. He thought of the guys down at the caravan park. Maybe there was somewhere to doss down there in one of the tents.

A four-wheel drive came up behind him. Stopped.

'Wanna beer?' Mac leant out the window. Grinned.

'Had one already.' This was a welcome face. 'Two. Could go another.'

'What's with the backpack?'

'Kicked out of the hostel.' Steve grinned back. 'Said I was trouble.'

Mac considered this for a second. Stared at the road ahead. 'Could put you up in the old man's bunkhouse, if you like. Not five-star, but okay.'

'Really?' Steve felt a wave of relief. 'I was wondering where I could shack up. Just for the night.'

'Stay as long as you like.' Mac leant across and opened the door on the other side. 'Like I said. Nobody uses it. Think Dad fixed it up for the dairy hand we never got.' Laughed. 'Got me instead.'

Steve went around and got in. Threw his backpack on the back seat. 'Thanks a million.'

'Reckon we might try a different pub tonight.' Mac shot a sideways grin at Steve. 'Somewhere you're not in trouble.'

'Maybe word travels fast here.'

'Not that fast, mate.'

27

Inside, the bunkhouse smelt musty. Everything covered in a layer of dust. Cobwebs stuck to the rafters. Still, better than the hostel.

Mac pulled sheets from a small cupboard. Helped him make up the single bed. Sniffed at the mattress. 'Smells okay. Not damp, I reckon. You should be all right in here. Come over to the house in the morning. Mum loves a new face. They'll be in bed now. Get up at the crack of dawn.' He grinned. 'Bloody cows. Twenty-four/seven job.'

Would his olds be as accommodating? Steve couldn't imagine it.

Next morning, Steve stood hesitantly in the doorway.

'Come on in, love. Did you sleep well? Knew the old bunkhouse would come in handy one day.' Mac's mother, middle-aged, permed brown hair, bibbed apron, stood at the stove. Skilfully flipped an egg onto a plate and handed it to Mac. 'Your father coming in soon?'

'Just cleaning up.'

'Better put on his bacon then. Never can wait.' She tonged rashers into the pan. 'Name's Billie. There's tea in the pot. Help yourself, Steve, love.'

Holy shit! If this was Mac's life, no wonder he was so laid back.

His father proved laconic. A huge man, he acknowledged Steve with a nod.

'Thanks a lot,' Steve began. 'I'm really…'

'Mac's friends are good blokes.' The older man interrupted him. 'Where's those eggs, Bill?'

'Coming up, Ed.' Billie set his plate down and winked at Steve. 'Didn't I tell you he could never wait?'

Steve wondered how he would get to work. 'Is there a bus goes past here?'

'Nah. Only the school bus. And that's gone this morning.'

'Old bike out the back, mate,' Mac said. 'Mine, but I don't use it.'

After breakfast, Mac showed Steve the bike. 'Help yourself. Got to go now.'

The tyres were flat but there was a pump.

He was early at the newsagency. Propped the bike against the wall of the shop.

Joe looked surprised. 'Must've heard the alarm this morning then.'

'Kicked out of the hostel. Stayed at Mac's. Lent me his bike.'

'Those mining guys?'

'Had it in for me, I reckon.'

'You must be making an impact.' Joe chuckled. 'Bit of an irritation, anyway.'

'Reckon we've got to be more than that.'

'Won't happen in a hurry, son.'

'Got ideas how to speed it up?'

Steve had thought about this as he lay waiting for sleep in the bunkhouse. His anger bubbled again at the memory of the night before. 'We ought to raid their bloody equipment. Show them.'

'Violence of that kind is not the answer.'

Steve knew the voice. Bent over the magazine rack, he hadn't seen Jim enter the shop.

He stood to face the artist. 'Don't see why not. They physically had me thrown out of the hostel.'

'Did they actually grab you?'

'No, but they intimidated the old guy who minds the place.'

'Intimidation is nasty but violence is worse.'

'So you're going to let them mine the island without a fight?'

'I didn't say that. I'll fight, but on my terms.' Jim picked up a news-paper. 'Anything new, Joe?'

'About Sandpiper Bay? Not today.'

'I'll have this anyway. And a lottery ticket.' Jim fished deep into his trouser pocket. Paid Joe and turned to leave.

His admonishment further inflamed Steve. He was about to challenge the old man but Jim's quiet authority subdued him. Temporarily. The saying 'Actions speak louder than words' had a special meaning for him now.

Later, Steve sought out Tracy. 'It's all very well being decent and kind. But we're not winning at the moment and we have to.'

Tracy stared at him for a second. 'So what's it to you, Steve?' She continued to stare. 'I mean, really. Why does it matter to you? You don't even live here. Never have.'

That was the same old question. Why did it matter? Well, he was in it now, wasn't he? Involved. Up to his neck. And, he realised, he seriously cared about what that bloody mining company might do.

<h1 style="text-align:center">28</h1>

'Can I leave the paintings with you, Bert?' Jim had a couple of canvases covered with an old blanket. 'Can't get into the hall till a day before. Bring them over in the tinnie a couple at a time.'

'Spose.' Bert eyed them with a mixture of suspicion and respect. Jim was apparently a well-known artist. Or so it was said. But it might be difficult to find somewhere to keep them. 'Dunno where I'll put 'em but.'

'They could go upstairs. In the lobby.' Tracy was putting on her apron.

'Anybody could nab 'em from there.' The publican was aware of the miners occupying the bedrooms along the corridor.

'There's the cellar.' Tracy wasn't going to give in. 'We could put them at the back of the barrels.'

'Damp down there.' Bert didn't begrudge Jim some help. The artist looked old today. Vulnerable. 'I'll find somewhere, Jim,' he said. 'Don't you worry. How many are there?'

'About thirty. Different sizes.'

Jim had discovered more paintings than he'd thought. He'd buried them away behind and under his bed and in the one or two cupboards he'd assembled over time. They'd not totally pleased him but there wasn't time to do more to them. The two he had been working on were still work in progress but, as usual, they were more promising than the discarded ones. It was always the same. Each new work initially held promise that was never fulfilled in the end. Didn't quite make it to the level he wanted. However, people still bought them, apparently. Amazing, really. Allowed him to live the life he wanted. And anyway, the purpose was different now. Much as he hated the idea, he needed publicity this time. Wanted masses of people to come and have a look at least.

He went to Madge's shop to use her phone. Could have used the pub's but he felt a bit too public there.

'Can I use your phone, Madge?'

'Course you can. Got to put money in but.'

Jim put in several twenty-cent pieces and dialled the number. Apparently, the gallery owner answered. Jim's words were interspersed with moments of silence when the gallery man had his say.

'G'day, Ray. Jim Masters here… Nah. Not about to ship stuff for you. What's that? Yes, o'course I've got canvases on the go. Not what I'm ringing about… I'm having an exhibition up here…thought you should know. Yes, o'course you can come. Be glad of the publicity. It's about the island…you know. Opens 7 December.' Jim hung up. 'Noah's coming up,' he said in tones that implied this was serious.

Madge didn't ask who Noah was. Guessed it was good news. For Jim, anyway.

The artist walked back down to the wharf with a lighter tread. He was going to be busier than he had been for years. People had to know how it was on Sandhill Island. Hopefully go and have a look for themselves. Understand what mining would do to the place. Perhaps he was just being stupid. Could he really capture the beauty of the island? Maybe people just wouldn't get it. But he had to try. It was his one chance to make the place known. So people would want it to stay the way it was.

He noticed the large motorboat was moored near the little beach. When he came closer, he saw the ramp. His eyes followed the deep indentations where wheels had sunk into the sand. Up the track, past his place. They disappeared among the trees. What were those bastards up to now?

He padded out to the surf beach. Saw the equipment. Dinosaurs ready to devour but asleep for now. He'd have to try to make sure they never woke up. He went back to his shack to work again. It was all more urgent now.

29

Some of them had managed to cadge a ride out to the island. Two boats hove to a couple of metres from the closest beach. Six of them waded through the shallows to the sands. They carried bulging packs, and water bottles hung suspended. This was an annual pilgrimage to the shrine of their sport. The rest of the year, they rode the surf wherever and whenever they could, in between bricklaying, welding or whatever they did to put food on the table. Come December, they packed their duffle bags and polished their boards before heading north. One or two of them had old vans but most of the guys had one-man tents and some arrived by train.

This morning was one of those sun-parched days when they just knew the surf would be good. Usually, they would ride the waves until the sun began to sink and their hair was salt-encrusted. The fishermen knew them and could usually be cajoled into taking them across the narrow strait. At the end of the day, the same fishermen would be invited into the caravan park for a steak and a stubbie or two and they'd talk beside the barbie into the night. These young men were seldom drunk or disorderly and the town was glad to see them return each summer like migratory birds. The oldest was probably no more than thirty-eight and each year they inducted a new member, usually around eighteen or so. Women generally came and went, were romanced and then shrugged off at the end of the season. One or two of the blokes had succumbed to marriage and either they no longer came or they brought their women with them.

The surfers passed Jim's shack in silence. They knew about him. Respected his desire for privacy. Once shot of his area, though, their voices rose high into the canopy of green.

The closer they got to their particular stretch of beach, the louder their voices became, until their excitement would have been palpable to the casual observer. It was where they knew. Their surfing Mecca. They had never wanted to stay overnight, although they had discussed the possibility at one stage.

'Shoulda brought our tents over,' said one.

'Nah. No bogs or water and anyway it's better to just leave it the way it is.'

'Belongs to the old guy,' another volunteered.

'In a kind a way.'

Now they crossed the wallum heath area, nature's garden where only wild flora would grow in the nutrient-poor sandy soil. The blue of the sea lay ahead. They could smell the salty froth.

Then of one accord they suddenly stood still.

What the hell?

Huge objects stood up like beacons. Eiffel towers rising out of the sand.

'Bloody shit!'

'Jesus!'

Now they moved cautiously in a line. As though approaching something that might explode.

As they walked over the last mound that led down to the beach, the full array of mining machinery lay before them. Silent monoliths stood or lay across the entire length and depth of the yellow sands.

'Fuck!'

The six of them could only stand in silent amazement.

30

'Some bloody bastards have got equipment all over the beach,' one of the surfers later told Bert. 'Who the hell are they?'

'Mining company. Sand mining.' Bert recognised some of the men who had assembled in the public bar. They came every year. Appeared as though out of nowhere on bikes, in kombi vans, old shiny chrome cars. They drank a bit, which suited him. Smelt of marijuana at times but otherwise decent enough. Most of them were big blokes. One or two had tats. They seemed intent on fishing or surfing. They stayed for the summer break and then disappeared again. As though on cue at the end of the long summer holidays. Where they went was none of his business. He never asked and they never volunteered.

'They're only mining along that stretch of beach? How long they gonna be there?'

'I think they're planning to start at the beach. Dunno how far they'll go in the end. Dunno how long they'll be around either.'

'I thought the old guy owned the island. What's he say about it all?'

'He don't own the island.' Bert wondered what had made them think that. 'Jim don't like the mining either. But nothing he can do. Government musta given permission. Nobody asked around here. We was just told.'

The men muttered among themselves. Were clearly unhappy with the idea.

Tracy had not yet gone home. She'd just pulled a beer that she placed on the bar. Smiled at the guy who'd ordered it. She took the proffered money and put it in the till. 'There was a meeting. They told us it would be good for the town. Would buy us a new footy clubhouse.' She spoke loudly then. Wanted all these guys to know. 'Don't believe it myself. Reckon they'd tell us anything so they could go ahead. Was a good bit of opposition but most people believed their promises.'

'That'll do, Trace.' Bert didn't want trouble. Never did business any good. 'They don't need to hear your views.'

Later, Tracy saw Steve walk past the pub. 'Back in a minute,' she said to Bert and left before he had time to object.

Steve was wheeling his bike, heading in the direction of Madge's shop. 'You going back to the farm now?'

'Planned to. Why?'

'Could you wait a while? I could ride with you. Mac's farm isn't far from my place.'

Steve hesitated. Tried to think sensibly. 'Reckon I should go right now,' he said. 'Help Mac, if I can.'

'So why you going to Madge's?'

'Want to ask her if she's heard anything new.'

'Jim's bringing his paintings to Bert's,' she said. 'Keeping them at the pub till his exhibition.'

'Oh.' Steve felt slightly miffed that Tracy knew things that he didn't. He swung a leg over his bike. 'I'd better go anyway,' he said. 'See you.' He gave a kind of salute before pedalling off.

Back at the pub, Bert was in conversation and merely nodded at Tracy. 'Where you go?' he asked. But he didn't seem annoyed and she merely grinned at him.

'Private matter, Bert,' she said, 'Sorry, but I was only gone a coupla minutes.'

The place was crowded now but she was suddenly aware of Andy. His eyes on her. A cat about to pounce. She ignored him. Turned to pull another beer for a guy waiting.

Even before she placed the full glass on the counter, she felt Andy's presence close by. Smelt him. For a millisecond she froze, then, deliberately ignoring him, went from behind the bar to collect some empty glasses at a nearby table. She had a glass in her right hand before she felt one of his hands grip her left wrist, pin it behind her back as he swung her round to face everyone while he stood behind her.

'You gonna give in soon, girlie,' he whispered before he released her and stepped away. He spoke loudly then. 'Tracy's a reliable girl, Bert. Aren't you, Trace?'

'Got a mind of her own, I'll say that,' Bert said and they all laughed.

Tracy was both afraid and angry. She still felt his hand on her wrist, hot, strong. She was no match for him and her fear was increased by that knowledge. Anger grew with this sense of impotence.

She wished Steve had waited for her when she went to get her bike from the rack. It was still light at six o'clock but the sulphur-crested cockatoos were circling and shrieking their evening cries. The sound, that evening, seemed like a warning. Perhaps they were watching her. She wouldn't put anything past those birds. Could eat the wood around window sills when they were in a mood for it. She inwardly smiled at the thought of how much their sharp cries echoed her own sense of frustration and fear of Andy. But she wasn't about to give in to him. Let him know she was afraid. Her feet felt for the pedals and she rode home in as leisurely and defiant manner as she could.

31

Steve discovered he had become used to waking at around six thirty in the morning. Had never managed to do that in Sydney. On this Sunday, he awoke as usual and lay listening for a few moments to the sounds of the farm. Cows with their comfortable mooing and the birds' cries. Sometimes the unmistakable warble of the magpie. He'd not thought before how appropriate that word was for describing the sound these birds made. He lay with his eyes shut, absorbing it all when he heard boots stomping their way across the yard.

Shit! Sunday was just another early start to Mac. He scrambled to dress.

In the farmhouse, Mac's mother was at her stove position in the kitchen.

'Hi ya,' Mac said when he saw Steve. 'Good day for surfing. Wanna come?'

'Sure.'

They scoffed down their breakfast, grabbed boards and stowed them into Mac's ute.

The journey was punctuated by stops as they let the good surf weather get around the district. A fine hot day to come on the one largely free day of the week. Needed no more words. The boards sticking up from the truck said it all.

They gradually assembled at the little beach. Boats of all kinds were dragged up onto the island before they almost silently began the walk to the surfing side.

There was no sign of Jim. Probably still in bed. Steve was tempted to stick his head in behind the sacking but remembered Jim's admonishment of the day before and thought better of it.

It was one of those days when the stillness emphasised the heat to come. Even the birds seemed to have gone to rest. The dirt under their feet was already warm.

When they came up over the little ridge at the end of the wallum heath, they stood stock still. They had known things would be happening but not to this extent.

'Holy shit!'

'Bugger-me-Charlie!'

'Fucking hell!'

The silent shining monsters seemed ready to devour everything in their path.

Steve and the others stood there for a minute or more. Silently, their eyes ranged over the beach. The roar of the waves seemed to make a mockery of their plans to surf. Not much room to move here now. One or two of them walked down the bank to take a closer look. Stood on the sides of equipment to peer at the inner workings.

The waves were perfect. It was close to high tide so not far to walk to the water. But somehow the joy of it had gone. The adrenalin drained.

'You reckon people know?' one of them shouted above the roar.

'Mining company sure does,' Mac shouted back. 'Dunno about people in general.'

'Jim knows.' Steve realised at that moment how Jim must feel. His rage. 'He tried to tell people at the meeting.'

For answer, they walked down past the machinery and into the water. They rode the waves for half an hour or so. Then wordlessly, and in unison, put their boards on their shoulders and walked back up the beach.

'Let's face it, Steve,' Mac said, 'We don't know exactly how much damage that lot will do. That machinery maybe makes it look worse than it's really gunna be, don't you reckon?

They stood still and Steve realised they were all looking at him. He had to give them an answer. Persuade them. 'Jim's idea is that they will damage the structure of the sand and the life that it contains.'

'You wouldn't think sand would contain that much life, though, would you?'

'But it must. Look at the way the heath plants grow on it.' Steve spoke as much to himself as to the others. 'And grow in it.'

'I guess it's kind of like a line of upright dominoes. When one falls over, they all do.' Rob spoke thoughtfully, then he looked at Steve. 'But how do we stop the first one from falling?'

They were not game to look at each other. Stared into space. A few seconds of silence.'

'Reckon we have to stand in front of those miners. Stop them working.' Steve spoke in a voice that didn't seem to belong to him.

One of the others laughed. 'Oh, yeah! Us against that lot.'

'Police come and we all end up in the clink.'

With consenting noises, they continued their walk back to the boats.

On reaching the sandy beach, they saw Jim in the distance. His boat appeared packed.

'He's setting up his exhibition,' Steve said.

'Suppose the poor old bugger is hoping to make some money. Can't have much. Soon, isn't it?'

'Opens Friday night, I think,' Steve said. He wanted to add that Jim was apparently quite famous. Probably had more money than he knew what to do with. But everybody had different views of the old man and at least these guys were sympathetic.

When they got back to land, there was no sign of Jim, although his tinnie bobbed beside the jetty. The guys muttered among themselves before loading their boards onto their various vehicles. Then the roars of utes faded into the distance.

Mac had loaded the boards into his truck. 'C'mon,' he said. 'We can enjoy a schooner at least.'

Steve wanted to find out what Jim was up to. Maybe see Tracy but then he remembered her aunt and uncle liked her to be at home on Sundays. He got into the cabin and Mac started the engine.

'We'll have to try find another surfing beach,' he said.

32

On Friday afternoon, Jim was given a key that gained access to the school's assembly hall. It was a fairly barren place with a stage at one end and stacks of chairs in front. The door and all the windows were down one side so the walls on the other side and at the end were bare brick. Jim had come prepared with suction-type picture hangers.

He was careful not to carry too many paintings at once because some of them were sufficiently large to almost obstruct his vision. He didn't want to trip at this crucial stage.

He stacked them against the end wall and went back to the pub to gather some more.

It was a slow and painstaking job. He knew enough about gallery exhibitions to fuss over where canvases should be hung. Joe had made a sign for outside. A banner tethered at each end. Easy to see, Jim thought.

Some of the paintings focused on trees on Sandhill Island, others were of scrub and yet others of the island's wildlife. As he hung them, he stopped at times, noticing things he could change even at this late hour. But he contained the itch and moved on. Time was of the essence. And he was tired. Had he ever felt so tired? He wasn't just *getting* old, he *was* old. Had never acknowledged it before. Not seriously. Now he knew but he pushed himself to set it all up as it should be.

Joe and Steve came in just after seven. They helped with the higher pictures. Steve stood on the ladder while Jim passed him the canvases. Madge arrived at eight with a casserole dish wrapped in an old blanket and a basket of bowls and spoons. The four of them pulled chairs from the stack and sat to eat the thick beef and beans soup.

Madge stared at the paintings. One in particular. Head on one side, she fixed her eyes on it. Eventually, she licked her spoon and sighed. 'I think I get it,' she said at last. 'Just kind of squiggles at first, but now I can see a tree. Kinda. In what looks like rain.'

'Love rain,' said Jim. 'Glad you can see it, Madge.' He gave a kind of mirthless laugh. 'Should get you to explain to the visitors.'

Madge took him seriously. 'Nah. Reckon they'll know more about it all than I do.' She smiled at him. 'Hope so, anyway.'

'I had a few people tell me they're coming,' Joe said. 'Got a phone call from some guy who said he was a journo from the *Herald*. Didn't give his name.'

'The more publicity the better.' Jim gave another chuckle. 'Never thought I'd hear myself say that. Publicity means people. Lots of them. Never been keen on that. Not till now.'

'Well, tomorrow's the day, Jim,' Joe said getting up. 'What time d'you reckon people will start coming in?'

'It says five on the flyer so I guess that's when it will all happen.' Jim yawned. 'Or not.'

He was not to know that word had already gone out through the media. Jim Masters, the famous artist, was no longer a recluse. Was having an exhibition. What had induced him to leave his hermit's life? To publicly display his work? Masters paintings were usually only seen in galleries down south. Arts editors spoke with their reviewers.

33

Madge had offered to make mini sandwiches and Bert had barbecued chicken on skewers. Jim had ordered fifty bottles of a prize-winning Hunter Valley sparkling wine.

'Holy shit, Jim. This's gonna cost ya,' Bert said, loosening the first cork.

'Yeah. Well.' Jim had seemed unconcerned.

'Two thousand dollars isn't chicken feed, Jim. You sure?'

Jim had laughed, 'We'll all get pie-eyed if not too many come then, won't we?'

But he was quietly hoping for big numbers. He wanted people to ask questions. Wanted to be able to tell them what was at stake.

Some of the big-city arts writers and reviewers had decided to drive and others to fly into Coffs on the opening day. Curious, some had contacted the gallery where Jim's work was usually exhibited. The gallery owner had clearly been briefed by his star artist and was now on his way north as well.

Steve had felt himself a member of a kind of exclusive club when Jim asked him to help set up the exhibition. Then he'd been given the task of sitting at the door on opening night and handing out catalogues as people came in. Joe had run off five hundred copies of the list of items on display. Seemed like an awful lot to everyone except Jim, who had suddenly acquired enormous confidence in the whole concept.

It was Joe who discovered the break-in next morning. Passing the school hall, he noticed the door half ajar. Surely they'd closed it the night before? Locked it, hadn't they?

He peered inside. It seemed a tsunami had ripped through the hall. Canvases were lying on the floor. One or two of the framed paintings had had their frames broken in several places so the paintings sagged within them. A couple of canvases were slashed with what must have been a knife.

'Bastards!' was all Joe could muster before going to the pub to alert Bert and to call the police.

A small cluster of locals appeared out of nowhere, curious and shocked.

'What happened?'

'Who'd do such a thing?'

'Sandpiper Bay's always been a safe place.'

'It's one of them visitors, I'll bet.'

By the time the police arrived, Joe was at the island alerting Jim.

With a sinking heart, he followed Joe's boat in his tinnie and walked with him to the hall. They stood in silence at the entrance. Joe felt an inward, immediate sense of panic. Then he calmed himself. How bad was it really? Not impossible, surely.

The police were asking people to stay outside. Were dusting frames for fingerprints.

Pinned to one of the posts outside the hall was a small piece of paper that caught Jim's eye. On it were the words 'Long live mining'. Jim surreptitiously removed it, pushing it into his pocket.

'Your exhibition was it, Mr Masters?' one of the policemen asked. 'Somebody didn't want you to go ahead, I'd reckon.'

'Apparently not.'

'D'you have any idea who might be responsible?'

Jim wasn't about to say so at this moment. He just wanted to get inside and fix what he could. There was no advantage to be gained in causing everything to come to a standstill while the culprit was apprehended.

When he was eventually allowed inside the hall, he stood for a moment to assess the situation. Two paintings were damaged beyond repair. Most needed only more cord or wire to rehang them.

Joe hovered. 'I'll get the stepladder for you,' he said.

'The hooks are still in place. I've got more cord in that box with the other stuff.'

They'd left everything in one of the dressing rooms at the back of the stage the night before. Thank God that door had been locked.

When Steve arrived at the newsagency, he found it still shut and no sign of his boss. One or two people were waiting outside but Steve told them he'd no key and would have to go to find one. He actually had no idea what to do and Madge wasn't open so he went to ask Bert if he knew where he'd find another key.

'Joe's up at the school hall,' Bert said. 'Been some damage done or something. Police are there.'

Up at the hall, Steve found two police cars with lights flashing. Inside, Jim and Joe were picking up canvases from the floor.

A policeman blocked his path. 'Can't go in there just yet, son.'

'But what's happened?'

It took Joe and Jim a good three hours to rehang the paintings. By mid-afternoon, it looked as though nothing untoward had happened.

34

Leaving Joe to mind the place, Jim went back to the island to clean up and dress for the evening.

He had fished out his one and only suit for the occasion. Smelling decidedly of naphthalene, it was outdated in both style and colour but all of that was of small consideration to Jim. He had always been fond of his dark red tie with orange stripes and that covered up the fact that some of the buttons on his shirt were missing. He even dug out his old silver cufflinks that had been kept in a shoebox along with his ancient lace-up brown shoes. A shame he had to go across in the tinnie. Difficult to seem pristinely tidy after that journey.

Whether the paintings sold or not was really of little consequence to him. It was the opening speech that was important. When he got to the hall, he made sure the school microphone was in place.

People began arriving soon after half past four and, by the time five o'clock came, the place was a mass of moving colour and voices. Steve was amazed by the people and the language. None of it fitted with either the old artist or the limited school knowledge he had of art. Where had all these people come from? They didn't belong with the locals at all. Seemed many of them knew each other.

'Lovely to catch up, darling.' Smack of lips on cheek.

'Where have you been for so long?'

'Christ it's good to see old Jim still going.'

'Just adore that shirt.'

Then someone got in front of the mic. A man with long hair and flamboyant jacket.

'Hmmm!' He cleared his throat and conversation gradually ceased. 'This is a special day. We haven't see Jim for a while. Gone into hiding they told us when we asked.'

Murmurs of agreement before a voice called out, 'He can't fuckin' hide.'

'We should have known he was just digging in for a while. And what a place to hide. This proves' – he waved his hand round the room – 'it has been a period of productivity far beyond his usual turnout. Perhaps we should all consider a reclusive life of this sort?'

Voices expressed agreement, laughter.

'But Jim wants to tell you how all this came about. So before I pronounce this exhibition officially opened, I think Jim should have his few words.'

Steve felt pride in the old man, with still a touch of the embarrassment of youth. Where had Jim got that ancient suit? Looked like something out of the ark. Probably had it stuffed in one of those old suitcases in his shack.

'Ladies and gentlemen – friends,' Jim said in that old man voice of his, 'thank you all for coming.' He looked at a man with a camera standing nearby and grinned. 'Good to see newspapers are represented here. I've got a message to send to the rest of the country. One we should all read about and need to deal with.'

Steve was momentarily almost blinded by the flashlight of a camera facing him.

Jim had pulled a piece of paper from his pocket and now glanced at it. 'We are at war in this country with those who want to plunder the beautiful environment.' He paused to allow the words to register. 'I have lived for the past five years on an island. A most lovely and unspoilt place…until now. You will notice my paintings here this evening represent aspects of nature. I've tried to recreate the life of the island. Sandhill Island. Trees, plants, animals, birds – they were around me every day and during the nights. I haven't actually been hiding. I've been living – in the real world. In a house I put together from whatever I could find.' He gave one of his chuckles. 'And those who know me well would know what that house would be like.'

There were comments of 'Can just imagine' and groans of 'Oh, my God.'

Jim smiled briefly. 'Yeah, well. It's my hidey-hole. Away from you lot.'

Much laughter.

'Just getting on with work. Trying to do justice to the sheer bloody beauty of the place.'

He seemed to almost dream off at that point and Steve wondered if someone should tap him on the arm, remind him of where he was.

But the old man straightened up and his voice became stronger. 'And now some want to destroy it all. Mine it for minerals. Have got machinery to dredge the dunes – the sand. Will suck up all that white mass and take out the goodness. Will cut down whatever is in their path. Trees, bush, animal shelters. It will all be gone by the time they finish with it.' Paused.

Steve was impressed by the way Jim had the audience in. Had them all listening intently. A lesson in making a speech, he thought.

'And this is the way it will all go. All our precious places. They will all disappear.' His voice dropped and he stared out into the crowd. 'Unless we stop them. Me and you. It's up to us to send out the message. No more messing with our land. Leave Sandhill Island alone. Let it be, just the way it has always been, in a hundred years for the kids of our kids.' He stopped again to let his words sink in. 'Now please enjoy my re-creation of this wonderful place. And…' he chuckled again, 'and spend some money so I can go on fighting the good fight.'

There was applause at that point and Jim turned to look straight at Steve for a moment. His eyes blazed with the unspoken words, 'See what I mean?'

Champagne corks popped and Steve found himself surrounded by people talking loudly and waving catalogues. He stepped back into a corner of the room, noticing that red stickers were on a few of the paintings.

He realised suddenly that two men, one with a camera, stood in front of him.

'So do you understand these paintings?' the man without the camera asked. 'As a young man, do they mean something to you?'

'No… Yes… I mean, I've been there,' Steve stammered. A thought niggled. Why was he afraid to speak out? Support Jim? He wasn't at home. He'd broken free of the old man. His life in Sydney. He could say what he bloody-well liked. He smiled. 'It's a hell of a place. Amazing, actually.'

'But surely mining can coexist?'

'Shit, no.' Steve didn't care at all now.

The camera clicked. Then a flash!

'No mining should be allowed. Ever! It'll damage the place – completely.'

'So what's particularly amazing then? Why is mining such a bad thing? Surely jobs are what's needed here.'

Steve's thoughts raced. 'Jobs do it only for a bit, I reckon. Sandhill Island should go on forever. If you look at Jim's – I mean Mr Masters's – paintings, they kind of say it. The trees and flowers and stuff.'

Another couple of men stepped forward. Again one of them held a camera.

'So you understand his paintings?'

Now Steve noticed a pad and pen in the hand of the one without the camera. Another newspaper guy?

'Nah. It's just clear to me. It's how it is.'

The man smiled, 'Well, I shall have to have another look then.

More flashes and clicks. Then the men moved off, but a third man now came to stand in front of Steve. He was beginning to feel under siege. He looked around to see Jim was being interviewed by the two blokes he'd spoken to before. How many journos were here, he wondered.

'You a good friend of Mr Masters, are you?' this reporter asked.

'I know him a bit. Met him on the island.'

'Do his paintings do justice to the place?'

The questions prodded and probed. Steve could only answer them as best he could, wondering if he was doing right by Jim.

'How does that feel?' Joe was at Steve's side. 'You'll probably be on tele tomorrow. In the newspapers.' Joe slapped Steve on the back. 'You told 'em. Good for you.'

At that moment, Steve felt much older than eighteen.

35

It was strange how different paintings looked when hung on pale-coloured walls. Flashes of colours that had appeared strange and indecipherable around Jim's shack now looked large and impressive on the walls of the hall.

People Tracy had never seen before held champagne flutes and spoke in loud voices, obviously familiar with each other. She rejected the offer of champagne and slipped between the chatting couples to stare at some of Jim's work. She still didn't understand any of them but, somehow, that didn't seem to matter. Each one said something to her and she felt a little proud that she could create such imaginings. *Ferns in rain* was one she stood in front of for a long time. The ferns weren't ones she'd recognise and it all looked dark to her. *Gloom* she would have called it but it didn't make her feel depressed. Instead, she was enjoying the different shades of greyish green.

There were two or three blokes with cameras and microphones talking to Jim and then Steve. They were on the far side of the hall from herself and she wondered what Steve was saying.

'So what do you make of these?' a man she didn't know asked her.

'Oh…I don't really know.' She was embarrassed by her ignorance but told herself not to be. 'I guess I see things that probably aren't what Jim intended.'

'So you know the artist personally?'

'Sort of.'

'Jim's a good bloke. I know him quite well. We shared a studio at one time. Not for long though. He was always fidgety. Wanted to see the world.' The man laughed softly. 'I gather he's finally settled now, though. Trust Jim to find some quiet island where he can be himself.'

'Sandhill is a great island,' Tracy said. 'Jim's built himself a place and he's happy there.' She looked round to see who was near. 'But the island will be ruined if sand mining goes ahead.' My little bit of protest, she thought.

'Well, I think people will want to go there just to have a look now. Jim's done a great job of promoting the place.' He turned as another man tapped him on the shoulder. 'Good God, man. I didn't expect to see you here.'

'Not every day Jim has an exhibition like this. I suspect a few chequebooks are already open.'

The two men moved off and Tracy saw Madge standing alone a little way off.

'What d'you reckon, Madge?' Tracy asked when she got close.

'Never have understood his paintings. Just a lotta lines and circles to me,' Madge chuckled. 'But I never learnt art. Not even at school.'

'I really like them,' Tracy said. 'Reckon you don't need to have learnt art. You can make what you want to of them, seems to me.'

'So now you can explain to me what you make of this one.'

They moved along the row, with Tracy giving her interpretation of the various items.

'Pity Bert couldn't come,' she said, after the last one. 'I offered to stay back so he could get a bit of a look but he said he was too busy now.'

'And he sure is,' Madge said. 'He's got bookings coming out of his ears. For this summer and next, he says. Seems suddenly everyone wants to know about the island. I've had lots of visitors ask me about where they can stay around here.'

Tracy laughed. 'Sounds good, Madge. Maybe we'll have to watch out for tourists rather than miners.'

36

The next day felt flat. To make it even more depressing, it was raining. Sunday. Mac said he had fencing to repair on the farm. Steve offered to help, but Mac said he and his father could do it. Were used to it and worked fast. Steve put on his wet weather gear to ride into town on his bike. Parked it outside the pub and walked towards the jetty. Wondered if there might be a boat going out. Felt he should go to see if Jim was all right after all the excitement. Maybe get to do some more painting himself.

Passing the camping ground, he caught a voice calling out, 'How'd the exhibition go?'

Steve recognised one of the guys who'd bunked down in a tent. Drove an old kombi van. He'd like one of those. They were cool. He could go all over the country if he had one.

'It was okay, I guess. Masses of people. Dunno who they all were.'

By this stage, the young man had come close. Steve noticed his hair was wet. Looked kind of stiff. Sea salt? Probably didn't do anything 'cept surf in the summer. How did he make his money? Must have to work the rest of the time.

'You going over to the island today?'

'About to see if there's a boat to take me.'

'Johnno's got a boat.' He turned to call out, 'Hey, Johnno!'

Another body emerged from another tent. 'Yeah. What's up?'

'Take us over to the island, mate. Just for a while.' The guy beside him turned back to Steve. Said conspiratorially, 'Let's go see what the mining bastards are doing, hey?'

Steve wondered what the guy had in mind.

'Okay,' Johnno said, coming towards them. 'No surf. Nothing much else to do in this fucking weather.'

Both of the guys had on board shorts and Ts. Rubber thongs. Hadn't shaved for a while. Sand had permeated every inch of their beings. Between their toes. In their fingernails.

'Steve,' said Steve by way of introduction.

'Chris,' said the guy closest. 'What you about, Steve? Apart from knowing the artist bloke?'

'Oh, just finding out how things tick,' Steve said. It rolled off his tongue so easily it sounded like he was totally in control.

'Let me know when you find out then,' said Johnno and laughed.

Chris laughed with him and Steve felt young and foolish.

'Come on, then,' said Johnno. 'Let's go.'

There was a kind of loping slouch to the way they walked. As though they had all the time in the world. Steve thought they looked cool. In his mind, he imitated them. They spoke laconically about the day and where they were headed.

'Let it go.' Of the rope that tied them to the jetty.

'Fuckin' wet.' Of the day.

'He there?' Of Jim as they passed his shack.

When they got to the surf beach, they stood totally still for a moment or two. Absorbed the black shapes of the machinery. Ominous and large.

'Fuckin' hell.'

The rain had become a fine spray, almost mist. Strangely, there seemed nobody around. Not even a dog.

'Reckon we oughta make some of these impossible to use for a while,' said Chris. 'Cut a hydraulic line.'

These guys seemed to understand the basic workings of what must be a dredger.

'Need something to do that with,' said Johnno.

'Could go find something.'

'Wouldn't take long.'

Without another word, the two turned and walked back towards their boat. Steve still stood where he was. Had he understood them?

He hesitated. His gut feeling told him this wasn't a good idea, that Jim wouldn't like it. But they'd said they'd only put the equipment out of action for a while. Wouldn't be wrecked altogether. Anyway, they mightn't find anything to use. Might – probably would – think better of it. They weren't bad blokes. Vicious. When he finally turned to follow them, he had to run to catch up.

As they neared the sandy beach, where the boat was moored, Jim appeared from his shack. 'What you fellas doing?' Jim's voice sounded calm but Steve detected an edge to it. The old man was slowly rolling a cigarette.

'Leavin' you alone, old man,' Johnno said not unkindly.

'And the island,' Jim said.

It wasn't a question. Steve knew that look.

'A shame the bloody sand miners haven't got the message,' said Chris.

'They will. In due course.' Jim sounded certain. 'You'll not get any-where by causing trouble.

'We haven't planned on big trouble.'

'Just leave it.'

The two guys were obviously surprised by this turn of events.

Jim struck a match and lit his cigarette. He inhaled and exhaled slowly 'Whatever you've got planned, I don't like it.'

The four of them stood still. Caught in the moment.

'Doesn't smell good,' he added. Then, 'Come on inside, out the wet.'

Johnno and Chris looked at each other, then laughed. 'No thanks, old man,' Johnno said. 'We gotta go. Come on, Steve.'

Steve was trapped. Should he go with them? Jim was clearly not im-pressed. He cursed himself, but hovered. He was an adult now. Could do what he bloody-well liked. And the guys hadn't done anything wrong. Yet, anyway. They just stood up for what Jim himself believed in. But the old man still looked as though they'd committed a crime. Steve had to get back to the mainland and these guys had a boat. He turned his back on Jim and followed them but he felt the artist's eyes watch him go.

37

Twenty-four hours later, Steve was at work when a familiar figure, one he had not expected to see, appeared in the newsagency doorway. It couldn't be him, could it?

'Dad!'

'Excuse me, but may I speak with my son?'

Joe smiled briefly. The expression was not returned.

'Outside,' said Bob Hastings, in tones that implied that he would not brook argument.

Joe was clearly surprised, to the point of speechlessness, but managed a nod.

They were hardly out of earshot before his father started to shout. 'Do you have any idea of the upset you have caused?' His old man's eyebrows were shooting up and down in agitation. 'Well, do you?'

Steve opened his mouth to reply.

'Utterly uncaring. Totally…selfish.' The veins on Bob Hastings's neck stood out. 'Your mother has been sick with worry and now… this…this…embarrassment.'

'What embarrassment?' Steve wasn't going to admit to anything.

His father's voice dropped, 'How do you think we found you? You were on the news. The bloody news. There you were saying things about this stupid little island that's caused such a stir. Channel bloody Nine. Not even the ABC. Might have been some dignity in that. But no, you had to stick yourself in the way of some inferior dickhead reporter. Tell them all about this bloody little island that nobody had ever heard of till all this…this fuss over mining it.'

'It's not a fuss.' Steve had found his tongue. Felt the old defiance surge. 'It's serious, Dad. They're going…'

'What is serious is that you've made us a laughing stock. An eighteen-year-old who runs away from school…a bloody good school… and shacks up with a dropout…a whole lot of dropouts. Time you got back to the real world, son.'

'Jim's an artist, not a dropout. He's famous, actually.'

This caused a second's pause.

'The bottom line is you have disgraced the family and upset everybody.'

Steve felt it important to call his father out on that one. 'Who, apart from you and Mum, have I seriously upset, Dad? Name some names so I get it, please.'

At a loss, his father could only mutter, 'Well, the school, the headmaster, your friends, relatives.'

'No doubt relatives will express shock, Dad. But I really don't care what the school thinks and I'm sure my friends would feel as I do…if they knew about it.'

'So our huge expense for you to attend a good private school means nothing to you?'

'Dad, you were the one who wanted it, not me. I would have been happy to have gone to the high school where most of the local guys went. But you didn't ask me, did you?' Steve saw the sudden anguish in his father's eyes and felt a moment of remorse. 'Not that I would have even understood at twelve years of age, I guess.'

Bob Hastings's shoulders seem to slump before a last-ditch attempt to assert himself. 'No, you wouldn't, so we made that really important decision for you. Dug deep into our finances and did without so you could have the best.'

'But you didn't ever do without, Dad. You know that as well as I do.'

There was silence as the two stared at each other.

Finally, his father said, 'I need a bloody strong cup of coffee.' He turned to look around for a likely provider.

'Madge serves coffee, Dad.'

Steve led the way to the little general store.

Madge's button eyes took them in and smiled. 'What can I do for you gentleman?' she asked. 'No need to ask if you're Steve's dad,' she said. 'Your son's a real chip off the old block, I reckon. A nice young man. Works hard, Joe says. Good manners too. Not like some.'

'Yes, well…I'd like a long black coffee,' Bob said. He fished in a trouser pocket for his wallet.

'Oh, this one's on me, Mr…Mr… Never did know your surname, son.' She grinned at Bob. 'Just pleased to see he's got a dad. Began to worry he might be all alone in the world…' Madge prattled on as she took out a mug and spooned instant coffee powder into it. 'And what do you want, Steve? Coke?'

Bob's anger had given way to exhaustion and for now the two men had run out of words.

Madge handed Bob his mug of coffee. 'Jim did real well out of his exhibition,' she said to Steve as she handed him a can of Coke. 'Sold a lot, I heard.'

'Did people understand why he was doing it?' Steve asked.

'Well he told them, didn't he? Reckon they must've.'

'So this is the artist you said was well known.' Steve's father sounded sceptical. 'Why would he have an exhibition here if he is so famous?'

'Oh, he's famous all right,' Madge said. Her pouter-pigeon look was beginning to assert itself. 'Youse better believe it. Lives on the island.' She snorted. 'The place they wanna mine.' She began vigorously wiping down the benchtop to emphasise her disgust. 'But Jim cares. He loves that island. All the creatures on it. And the plants. That's what his exhibition was all about. He says the place'll be destroyed by them mining lot. And I reckon he's right. Company called MinWorx.' She stopped rubbing and leant over the counter to glare at Bob Hastings. 'Lying lot, they are. Say they'll do no damage. But we all know the place'll never be the same again.'

Steve suspected his father was feeling undesirably involved in Madge's obvious antipathy towards the mining company.

'I can see you're worried about it,' Bob Hastings murmured.

'Worried! And I'm not the only one. Course some's more interested in jobs but they don't understand. Anyway, there are jobs here if they're prepared to work and maybe go somewhere else to get them.' She waved her cloth dismissively. 'I hear there's gonna be another meeting.'

'Who with? Because of Jim?' Steve was excited now at the thought that Jim's art might have stirred this up.

'Dunno. Some guy from the campsite told me.'

Steve wondered about this, as the camping guys hadn't struck him as an organised lot. Anyway, Madge might have got it wrong. He'd ask Joe when he got back to work. Work! Joe must be wondering why he was away for so long.

He glanced at his father. 'Should go back to work, Dad,' he said.' Joe will be wondering where I am.'

'What time do you finish?' his father asked.

'Six o'clock.'

'I'll be there,' his father said. 'We need to talk some more.'

38

Joe didn't seem to know about any proposed meeting. He was glad to see Steve return but was preoccupied with dealing with lottery tickets. The butts had to be in at Bucca by midday. Three times a week it necessitated a trip into the larger town, when Steve had to look after the shop for a couple of hours. Initially, Joe had been concerned about this but necessity overrode reservations. Fortunately, it was generally at a time when the shop was not overly busy. Anyway, after a week or two, he'd discovered that he could trust Steve.

Bob was waiting outside the shop when Steve left just after six.

'Catch you tomorrow,' Joe said, in such a way as to make it sound like a question.'

What did he think of Bob Hastings's sudden appearance? He had only asked, 'Was that your old man?'

'Yes.' Steve had tried to look unconcerned. 'Dad has just come up to check Sandy Bay out.'

'Worried about you, is he?'

'Nah. Just wanted to give the place the once over.'

As soon as he saw Steve, his father asked, 'Where you staying?'

'I'm living on a farm.' That sounded better than a hostel and the old man need never know he'd been kicked out of there. 'Where you sleeping?'

'I've booked into a motel in Coffs Harbour. My car's parked just near here.'

There was a moment of awkward silence. At least his father seemed calmer.

'Want to get something to eat?' Steve asked. 'The pub serves meals.' He'd held out the olive branch, which made him feel as if he was in charge. Up to the old man now.

'Is that where you usually eat?'

'Nah. I eat anywhere. Sometimes at the farm, often at Madge's. Wherever.'

'Guess we'll make it the pub then.' Bob Hastings managed a smile.

Bert was serving customers and only gave a wave as the pair made their way to the dining room. It was a fairly gloomy space with red-velvet flowered wallpaper and it smelt of onions. There seemed to be nobody else around. One of the kitchen staff came out to thrust menus in front of them. There wasn't a huge choice. Soup of the day, followed by pork chops or corned silverside with mashed potatoes and peas. Still, it looked pretty good to Steve, who hadn't eaten since his early breakfast.

'Where's the farm?' Bob Hastings asked.

'About twenty minutes by bike. That's chained up near the shop.'

'Your bike, is it?'

'On loan.' Steve had decided there would be no lying or pretending. That was what his father did. He wasn't going down that road. 'It's Mac's but he doesn't use it.'

'So who's Mac?'

'The son of the farmer who's letting me stay in his shed.'

'Shed? Is it comfortable?'

'It's cool. Like it's my own room.' He could afford to expand a little. 'I'm away from the house but I have my own bathroom. Was supposed to be for someone else but nobody ever really needed it.' He smiled. 'Till I came along.'

'Nice people usually. Farming people.'

'They're really nice. Billie cooks me breakfast. Along with her husband and Mac.'

'I'd like to meet them.'

There was another pause. Steve fidgeted with his knife and fork.

His father turned to look out the window beside them. 'Like something to drink?' he asked.

Steve was tempted to say he was sure his father was dying for one but refrained. 'Just a Coke, thanks.'

Bob Hastings returned with a beer and a double Scotch along with the Coke. The food arrived almost simultaneously. In almost companionable silence, the two tucked into their chops.

Steve allowed his father to pay for them both. Bert served Bob with another double whisky.

'Good bloke, your son,' Bert said. 'Works hard, Joe says.' He gave Bob a conspiratorial wink. 'Like father, like son, eh?' He leant forward and spoke quietly. 'Don't care for him much down at the hostel but.'

'Oh? Why's that?' Steve's father leant towards the hotelier.

'It's them mining lot.' Bert jerked his head towards the ceiling. 'Staying here at the pub too. Persuading us all that mining is good for us.' He shook his head. 'Not so sure, meself. They'll all be in later for a meal and a drink.'

'But why has Steve fallen foul of them?'

'Been too outspoken. Made friends with the artist bloke and them as what's against it.' He laughed. 'You that way too or did you just teach him to stand up for himself? Make waves?'

The foreheads of the two older men were almost touching.

'Well, I've always hoped he'd be able to give as good as he gets.'

The two men chuckled.

'He sure does that. You should be proud of him.'

'I've got to get going, Dad.' Steve felt he should save his father from having to avoid the reply Bert was obviously expecting. 'See you tomorrow, if you want, okay?'

'Sure.' Bob was looking flushed and his second double whisky was disappearing fast. 'I'll ring your mother later. Tell her you're alive.' He turned back to Bert. 'The young never keep their parents informed. You got kids?'

'Never settled long enough.' Bert leant further forward.

Steve could tell it would be a long night.

'Had a couple of birds though. Nearly married both times. They both wanted kids. Frightened the shit out of me.'

The two men were chuckling like a couple of kids as Steve walked out the door.

<h1 style="text-align:center">39</h1>

When he got back to the farm, he found Mac sitting in the near dark on the veranda.

'Hi,' Steve waved and called. Leant his bike against the bunkhouse wall. Walked towards the house. 'What you doing out here?'

'Unwinding,' Mac said. 'Been a hard day.' His eyes held Steve's for a moment. 'You know those guys at the campsite?'

'A bit.' Steve didn't want to talk about the way he'd followed them home. Had ignored Jim's warnings.

'Well, knowing them, even a bit, might not do you any good in the long run. I heard they're riled up against the mining lot.' Mac said. 'Not alone in that.' He smiled. 'But we all got to calm down. I think the miners will get the message. Eventually. Could take time but in the end they'll see that mining is not a good idea. Now the newspapers have got hold of it. Doesn't put them in a good light, does it?'

'But the guys at the camp, if they did anything stupid, would only make things worse. Is that what you're saying?'

'They could be trouble, mate.'

'Jim told them to forget doing anything. I heard him.' Steve sat wearily on the bed. Remembered Tracy's words. 'What does it matter to you?' He'd realised then that it did matter to him and now here he was, deep in the thick of it. More than he'd ever intended, anyway. And to top it all, his old man was around.

'I was with them when they saw the beach and the equipment,' Steve said. 'They were really angry. Said someone should put a stop to it. I didn't think they'd seriously do anything, though. Jim told them not to.'

'And they listened?'

'Well, they didn't pay much attention to him, I guess, but then they didn't seem likely to seriously do anything either.' His naivety suddenly overcame Steve. 'Oh, shit! And the old man's suddenly arrived.'

'Today?'

'Yes. Really mad at me. Still, nothing new in that.' He smiled rue-fully.

'Sorry about that but that's just olds for you. My old man doesn't put up with what he reckons is crap either. Not always easy.'

Steve had difficulty getting his head around the idea that Mac's father could be difficult. After a moment or two, he asked, 'What d'you do when he's mad?'

'Ride it out. Usually.' Mac laughed. 'Let him swear and cuss. Makes him feel better.' He stood up. 'He gets over it.' He chuckled again. 'They're just words, anyhow. We all of us say things we shouldn't at times.' He looked at Steve. 'Or don't say things we should.'

Steve, still standing on the veranda steps, felt a wave of guilt. He shouldn't have gone along with the camping guys. Should have stayed with Jim. Backed him up. He saw that now. 'Reckon that's the hardest thing,' he said now. 'Not saying what we should.'

'Yeah, well…don't worry about it. Just thought you should know what's what. Those camping guys have laws unto themselves. Haven't done anything so far but I reckon they could cause trouble. Thought you should know,' he said. He yawned and stretched. 'Turning in now, mate. See you.'

Steve went inside to the comfort of his cabin. Lay on his bed and thought about it all. He could see now that he'd behaved like a kid. Hadn't backed Jim up when he said there should be no trouble. But why should he back the old artist? Because he owed him. That was why. Those pictures wouldn't do any good, though. Maybe there was only one way to make a point. But if those camping guys did damage to the equipment, they'd go to jail. If they were caught. But maybe they wouldn't be. He sighed. Why had he got himself into this mess, anyway? In the end, what on earth did it matter what happened on the island?

But it was a beautiful, unspoilt place. And he really liked Jim. What he said usually made sense. Those guys at the camping ground felt strongly about the island too, didn't they? For them, it was really only about surfing, not the island itself. Come to that, the mining company wasn't worried about the island either. Only Jim really cared.

'What does it matter to you?' He remembered Tracy's words and thought, not for the first time, that it actually mattered in a great many ways.

40

Sergeant Peter O'Leary had a bad feeling in his guts. Five years to retirement and, until then, he just wanted a quiet life. He and his wife, Olive, had bought a neat little house with a garden between Coffs and Sandpiper Bay. He'd joined the local bowls club. Life generally looked good for them. But now he felt as though he wasn't as in control of his life as usual.

The old artist's painting show had all the hallmarks of real trouble. Canvases had been scattered everywhere. Just bloody lucky none had been seriously damaged. He thought about who might be responsible. Of course, the anti-mining group was strong and no doubt caused ill feeling. Jobs right now were in short supply up around Coffs. Especially for the young and unskilled. Two opposing forces could doubtless generate bad feeling. But Sandpiper Bay had never been that sort of place. Farming community mostly. Law-abiding, hard-working people. Dependable. Predictable. That was what had attracted him to the area in the first place. No frills, but solid. He sighed.

There were no clues as to who might be responsible for this vandalism. That's what it was.

He'd left his men to watch over the hall and had gone to chat with the publican. A good starting point, he reasoned. Alcohol loosened tongues and the pub was where men talked.

'Hear anything about the exhibition?'

'Like what, Pete?'

'Like someone might not want it?'

'Nah. Not really.' Bert paused. Stared into space. Then grinned at O'Leary. 'Reckon the mining lot wouldn't like it, though. Not if they understood the exhibition was a kind of protest.'

'And is it?'

'Way I see it, it is.'

'How's that then?'

'The old artist bloke – Jim. He's tryin' to make people see the island as a lovely place. With his paintin's.' Bert rubbed his nose. Leant towards O'Leary. 'Only been over there to see the paintin's once, meself. No time when you got a pub to run. Dunno whether Jim's right. I'm not much into art.' He turned to where Tracy was drying glasses. 'You heard anything, Trace?'

'Not really,' she said. She didn't like coppers much but O'Leary seemed nice enough. 'I know there are some who want the mining to go ahead but some who don't like it at all.'

'So neither of you have heard any gossip?'

'Sorry, but I haven't.'

Tracy shook her head as Bert said, 'Would tell you if I had.'

'Well, you let me know if you do, will you?'

'Sure.'

'Meantime, I guess I'd better go see what these paintings are like.'

As O'Leary walked back to the school hall, an old VW Kombi rumbled past.

A radio blared and a voice yelled, 'Go catch 'em, copper.'

And another voice from within shouted, 'Bastards,' followed by laughter.

The sergeant felt, rather than heard, the animosity. It was in the air. Like the germ of a disease. He'd have to make sure they were all on alert. This particular disease could become a full-blown epidemic if they didn't watch out.

41

The next day, it was quiet in the small town. Time and again, Steve wondered if he'd see the police but there was no sign of them. What had they done about the damage to the paintings for the exhibition? Why weren't they asking questions? But there was no sign of them or Jim or even the guys from the camping ground.

It wasn't a day when he was needed late at the newsagency. At five o'clock, he went down to see if there was a boat going out. As he passed the camping ground, he noticed one of the guys who'd gone to the island with him was polishing his board. He looked up and waved at Steve. It all seemed quiet and as though nothing had happened. Weird.

There was a large crabbing boat about to leave the jetty. He found a perch between the piles of pots and jumped off when the fisherman got close enough to the island.

'Thanks,' he called back as he began the wade ashore.

There was no immediate sign of Jim. Steve went to the entrance of the shack and called out.

There was the sound of heavy breathing and a cough. Steve waited for a few more seconds and then lifted the hessian and went in.

Jim was a mound on the bed.

'You all right, Jim?'

The old man sat up. 'Course.' He flung his legs over the side of the bed. 'What you doing here at this hour?' The artist looked decidedly old, his neck had the stringy appearance of age, his arms and legs were thin, like sticks, and his eyes seemed cloudy.

'I thought you'd be working.'

'Hmmph! Have been but called it a day now. Tired after the show.' Jim reached for his packet of tobacco. He stared at Steve. 'You should steer clear of that surfing mob.'

'Which surfing mob?'

'Those camping-ground idiots. They can be trouble, Steve.'

'Everyone says that but I haven't seen them making any. Not so far anyway.'

Jim pulled out a cigarette paper and began to pile it with tobacco. Steve still stood watching him, not really knowing what to say or do.

'Maybe not yet. Reckon they could, though.' Jim struck a match and lit his cigarette. Sucked on it. Coughed.

'They might not.'

Jim shook his head. 'I certainly hope they won't. If they do, it'll make everything really serious. For everybody.'

'How d'you mean?'

'We'll be seen as stopping at nothing to have our way. And that means they'll be more aggressive about getting what they want.'

The words were not lost on Steve. Aggression created aggression. Violence led to violence.

'So how can we calm everybody down?' he asked.

'Just go home, son.' Jim spoke gently, but firmly. 'Don't get in-volved. It could turn nasty. Nastier, that is. You've done your bit.' He stood and Steve noticed he had difficulty. Jim grabbed the back of the chair by the bed. Grunted.

'Are you hurt?'

'I'm fine. Just old.' Jim smiled.

'You sure?' Steve didn't honestly know what he'd do if the old man wasn't okay.

'Absolutely, son.'

They stood staring at each other in silence for a few moments. The old man reached for a shirt and Steve turned towards the entrance.

'I should go now anyway,' he said. 'My old man's here.'

'Is that good for you?

'Better than it was when I left Sydney.' Steve realised at that moment just how much better it had been last night.

'Get on, did you?' Jim smiled. 'Talk?'

'Yes, we did actually. It got better as we spoke.'

'Always the same, son. Talking calms everything down.' Jim pulled his bottle of rum from the box under the bed. Unscrewed the top. 'Like to meet your old man,' he said.

'Not sure how long he'll be here but I guess long enough for that to happen.'

'Goodo.' Jim reached for his mug. 'Staying in Sandpiper Bay, is he?'

'Na. In Coffs. Said he'd be over again in a couple of days. Meeting up with some old mates of his tomorrow, apparently.'

Jim pulled one of Steve's recent drawings from the pile on his work table. 'This needs a bit of work on perspective,' he said. 'Good enough to warrant correction.'

Steve felt the glow of pride that Jim saw some hope in his endeavours.

'See here. This line needs to go further…'

The two of them were quickly engrossed. The sound of men's voices and the glow of torches finally penetrated their concentration.

'What the hell?' Jim stood still, paintbrush in hand.

They both listened. Heard the voices pass before Jim moved to the door. He briefly saw the silhouettes of figures.

'What you doing?' he called out into the night.

When there was no immediate response, Jim jerked his head to indicate they should follow the sounds. Grabbing his torch, he left the cabin. Steve followed and together they pounded silently down the track.

42

Tracy had seen Steve with the older man she assumed was his father. They hadn't looked too happy, either of them. They'd gone down towards Madge's but she lost track of them after that.

Now it was Thursday and almost midday. The pub was filling up with locals and some tourists who were looking for a pub lunch. The old guy, George, who liked to be called a chef but was hardly even a proper cook, was busy with the usual fare of steak and chips or curried prawns and rice.

It was at these busy times that Tracy quite enjoyed her job. She pulled beers, listened to men's stories and was kept abreast of the life in the small town.

'Me missus is due next week,' one of the younger farmers announced. 'Won't be in fer a while.'

'Going to be chief cook, are you?' Tracy said sympathetically.

'Nah. Ellen's mother's coming for a month.' He pulled a face. 'She'll enjoy it, looking after the kids, but I'll have to be on me best behaviour.'

'Ah well, a month's nothing really.' Tracy handed him his beer and smiled, before he went to stand further from the men round the bar.

The two who took up his place were men who were staying at the pub. Mining men wearing yellow T-shirts with MinWorx embroidered in black on their chest pockets.

'Not working today?' she asked. 'Or just a break for lunch?

'Nah. Start the big job tomorrow. Got the go-ahead at last.'

'Waiting for something, were you?' She didn't want to appear too nosy but in fact was more than curious.

'We weren't waiting for anything. Just the boss held up for test results.'

'So now you can start mining?'

He nodded his eyes on her over the froth of his beer. He stopped drinking and ran his tongue over his lips. 'Going over first thing.'

'Ah!' Tracy didn't want to go on with this conversation. Felt somehow disloyal just talking to this man. She must warn Jim. Steve.

When she knocked off, she told Bert she was going to tell Joe about the mining.

Bert nodded. 'Reckon them as against it won't be pleased. Won't do any good, though. What's gunna happen will happen.'

Joe was getting ready to close up.

'Where's Steve?' Tracy peered behind the newsagent.

'Gone home.'

'Already?'

'It's gone six. He finishes five thirty. Five if I don't need him. Met up with his old man tonight. Dunno where they went.'

'They're gunna start mining tomorrow,' she said.

'Jim won't like that.'

'Why I wanted to tell Steve. He could go over.'

'I'll tell him tomorrow, love.'

Tracy realised Joe didn't get it. Didn't understand how Jim would cope. What the old man might do.

She went down to the campsite. Someone there might care. Might go over. Warn the old artist.

But there didn't seem to be any of the surfing crowd there. Only families. Getting ready for the nightly barbecues. Kids were squealing. Chasing each other.

There was a teenager sitting with knees bent outside one of the tents. She was smoking and twiddling a strand of her long brown hair.

'You seen any of the guys?' Tracy asked.

The girl looked up at her. 'Nah,' she said. 'They've all gone over to the island.'

Concern gripped Tracy. 'What they go there for? Surfing?'

'Nah.' The girl drew on her cigarette. Exhaled slowly, her eyes screwed up from the smoke.

'So, what?' Tracy wanted to slap her.

'Dunno. Took some things with them and went off.' She laughed suddenly. 'Been smoking weed all afternoon.'

'What things?'

'Dunno.' The girl thought for a second. 'One of them said somethin' about bolt cutters.'

'Bolt cutters! You sure?'

'Pretty sure.'

Tracy felt a sense of panic. Bolt cutters could only mean one thing. She must warn someone. Stop the surfing guys from doing anything foolish. She muttered her thanks and went out into the street again. Supper time. Unlikely anyone would be around at this hour. There would be people in the pub, though.

In one corner of the bar, she saw Mac with two of his mates.

'Seen Steve?' she asked when she got close.

Mac turned and grinned. 'Well, look who's here,' he said, then seeing her expression added, 'No, I haven't seen Steve. But his old man's in town so I reckon he's caught up with him.'

'I need to talk,' Tracy said.

'Talk away…'

'Outside.' She didn't want to attract attention if it was all only in her imagination. And if it wasn't, she didn't want to cause any more fuss.

Mac looked puzzled but followed her to the door. His mates gave wolf whistles and there was derisive laughter.

'It's the surfing guys down at the camping ground,' Tracy explained as soon as they were out of ear shot.

'What about them?' Mac was serious.

'They've gone over to Sandhill and taken bolt cutters.'

'Shit! How do you know?'

'Girl at the camp site told me. They'd been smoking marijuana, she said. I'm scared they want to do some real damage and Jim won't be able to stop them. If he even sees them, that is.'

'Probably nothing, Tracy,' he said. 'But maybe we should go over. See what they're up to.'

'I'll go and see if there's anyone who might take us over. A bit late, but you never know.' Tracy turned to run to the jetty.

'Be there in a minute,' Mac called after her before he went into the bar again and spoke in low tones to his mates.

Then they followed him out and down to the jetty, where Tracy was talking to one of the fishermen.

As Mac and his little group approached, she said, 'Custer's going out.'

Mac looked down at the older man, 'Can you take us to the island? Beach near Jim's place? We can get ourselves back.'

'She's only thirty feet, mate. Might be room but.' Custer glanced at Andy, who was bent over the storage hatch, then said, 'Yous'll have ter perch where you can.'

The four of them stepped down from the jetty and the little fishing boat bobbed frantically.

'She's bloody low in the water,' Andy said, his eyes running over Tracy, who looked away. Then he leapt off the boat and untied it from its bollard before hopping back on board.

Not a word was said as Custer started the motor.

The island was a dark shape ahead in the twilight.

43

Bert knew suddenly what this latest development meant. Up till now, mining had been an amorphous image in his mind. Machinery, men, sand flying up into the air. The word 'dunes' had, in some strange way, made it real. Immediate. Tracy was a good girl. If she was alarmed enough to go to see Joe, it must be a worry for her. Probably should be for him too.

He saw her walk down the street towards the jetty, disappear into the camping grounds. Saw her come back and talk to Mac and his mates in the bar. Then they all went off. They seemed in a hurry. What was going on? There was nobody he could ask. Couldn't leave the bar to find out either. 'What time you start tomorrow?' he asked one of the MinWorx men.

'Sparrow fart, why?'

'You could be in for a bit of a stand-off, I reckon.'

'Them enviro idiots wouldn't dare.'

'Just a warning. Be on your guard. Nobody wants a real fight.'

The miner stared at the publican for a second, then went to the phone near the door.

Bert wondered if he should have alerted him but surely it would be better to stop any proposed damage before it happened. The mining company did have the law on their side.

He pondered for a while as he served customers. Chatted in an absent-minded way. He remembered O'Leary's words. Went to the phone.

'Hello, sarge,' Bert said a few seconds later. 'Reckon there's some trouble brewing on the island, maybe. Dunno for sure, but…they start mining there tomorrow. The real deal… Goodo.' He hung up, glad that weight had been lifted from his mind. Up to O'Leary now.

44

It was already night and even the light of the half moon was largely obliterated by the trees as the group pounded silently along the track towards the mining beach. Jim, holding a torch, followed them with Steve just behind. The smell of rotting vegetation, mixed with the dampness and sounds, was magnified. It was a place where whispers seemed more appropriate than voices.

As soon as they entered the wallum heath, the leading group could hear voices. Laughter.

Arriving at the crest of the dunes, they looked down onto the beach, where the machinery lay in darkness.

Jim and Steve finally came level with the others.

'What the hell…?' Jim's old man voice couldn't be heard above the waves and the shouts of the silhouetted black creatures climbing all over the sleeping dinosaurs.

Mac and his mates ploughed down through the soft sand.

'Don't do something stupid,' Mac called to the climbers. 'You could end up in jail.

'Got to be stopped,' one of the surfing guys yelled back. 'Now!'

'But not this way.'

'At least it'll slow the bastards down.'

'Just come down while we talk.' Jim was closer now. Seemed to have found his younger man voice. 'Not asking too much.' He sounded persuasive.

The guys on the machinery hesitated.

'Come on. Let's find the best way to deal with this.'

One of the surfing guys began to climb down slowly. The others watched before following suit.

'This needs to be thought through,' Jim said as the small band gathered around him. 'What damage have you done?'

The surfing guy, Chris, still looked defiant. He grinned. 'They might have trouble trying to start their motors.' He turned to look at his mates, then back at Jim. 'Actions speak louder than words, old man.'

'That's as may be,' Jim said. 'Depends on what sort of actions. You're only going to make matters worse with what you have apparently done already, young man.'

It dawned on Steve that this was another of those moments. He tried to make himself feel strong. Independent. 'You should listen to Jim,' he said. 'He…he…talks sense.'

'Not always, kiddo.' Johnno spoke then. 'And you're still too wet behind the ears to know anyway.'

Anger rose up but Jim laid a restraining arm on Steve.

'This is getting us nowhere,' Mac said. 'Let's decide the best thing to do now. Can you rectify your damage?'

'Not easily. Take time.' Johnno sulked.

'Surely one of you has the knowhow.'

'I think I could do it,' said Chris, sounding almost enthusiastic. As though it was a challenge he'd enjoy. 'You'll have to shine the torches up close so we can see.'

He began the climb back up, on one of the huge diggers, followed closely by the rest of his group.

The half moon failed to give as much light as they needed. Mac and Steve held torches, shining them on the place where the men were.

There were a few minutes of comparative quiet with only the sound of mutterings and the clank of metal on metal as they worked.

Suddenly the sound of motorboats and bright lights bore down on the beach.

The onshore group froze.

They watched in amazement as the boats rode over the waves and slid up onto the beach. Men leapt over the sides. Strode up the sand.

One called out, 'What the hell do you think you're doing?'

'Trespassers!' yelled another.

'Stay right where you are!'

Jim stood his ground. Said, 'We're aware of…'

He had no time to complete his sentence. One of the men grabbed him and held him with his arms behind his back.

'Hey!' Mac said. 'Leave the old man alone. He's done nothing wrong.'

A large bloke who appeared to be the leader of the group said, 'Drop everything!'

A wrench fell with a clatter, hitting metal before thumping into the sand. At that same moment, Chris and Johnno jumped from the machinery and onto Jim's assailant. One of them threw a punch that caught the man on the chin. This sent him flying and the full force of his weight toppled onto Jim, who fell awkwardly, landing with a grunt. Mac moved to assist Jim but was punched on the jaw by another mining guy.

It had become a muddle of men as the surfers, Mac, and his group fought indiscriminately with the miners. Steve saw Andy among them, which further drove his fury. Bastard! He could taste blood in his mouth. Sand flew up from pounding feet.

Tracy kicked out. Connected with a bloke's crutch. He yelped and doubled over. The air thickened with gasps. Steve found he had strength he'd never known before.

Moments later, he was made aware of another force.

Several policemen stood above them at the top of the closest dune.

'You buggers stop. Now!' a voice boomed.

Looking up, one or two of the group saw the police. Now they stood still, panting in silence. They were all cowed for the moment. Jim was still on the ground but struggling to stand.

'Dunno what you think you'll achieve by this sort of behaviour,' the sergeant of police said as he came down the bank.

'We were just trying to protect private property,' one of the miners said sulkily.

'Yeah, but that's not the way to do it.' The sergeant was not going to relent. 'I'd like you all to stand where you are right now and Constable Roberts will take down names and addresses.'

Steve was looking at Jim, whose continued struggle to stand was not proving effective. He tried to catch the constable's eye. 'Jim's been hurt,' he said. 'Looks like he's in real trouble.'

One of the policemen bent to assist Jim but the old man only groaned and fell back.

As the two constables assigned to the job moved among the group, the men reluctantly gave their names.

When he got to Tracy, the constable raised one eyebrow. 'What you doing here?' he asked. 'No place for a woman.'

'I'd like to help Jim,' she said. 'Get him back to his place.' She eyeballed the policeman. 'He lives on the island.' She pointed with her thumb over her right shoulder. 'The other side.'

The constable looked at the sergeant. Caught his eye with a questioning expression. The sergeant nodded.

'See what you can do then,' the constable said. 'The old bloke shoulda had more sense than to get caught up in all this.'

'He didn't want this to happen,' Tracy said as she moved towards Jim, who was still on the ground. 'Can someone help me get him up?'

'You help her,' the sergeant said to Chris, who was closest to him. 'Let's see if you can be of use for once.'

'Okay, Jim,' Tracy said gently as she and Chris bent to half lift the artist, who stood with difficulty, before they propped him up on either side.

The two of them half dragged and half carried him up the dune and along the track. He seemed almost unaware of what was happening and put up no resistance, struggling to put each leg in front of the other in an awkward gait. But Tracy noticed his breathing was harsh and obviously an effort.

The sounds of the sea and the men were soon left behind. Tracy was conscious only of the semi-dark and the old man's breathing.

'You're doing fine,' she said. 'Not too much further.'

There was in fact quite a way to go but she figured Jim needed encouragement. In spite of his age and shrunken stature, he was remarkably heavy, so it was a struggle to hold him upright as well as to keep moving.

When they finally reached the shack, they laid Jim on his bed and Tracy gently felt the damaged leg.

'Anything broken?' Chris asked.

'I don't think so. Probably just a bad sprain.' She looked down at the old man who had his eyes shut. 'You feeling okay now, Jim?' She noticed his breathing was still not good.

'She'll be right,' he said hoarsely. 'Bit of a pain in my chest. It'll go now I'm home.'

Tracy wasn't so sure. She looked at Chris. 'Reckon we should get him into hospital,' she said. 'Just to make sure.'

Jim opened his eyes wide and glared at her. 'I'm not going anywhere,' he said.

'And I'm not going to leave you here like this.' Tracy spoke firmly and Jim gave a twisted smile.

'Could do with a cuppa.' he said. 'There's tea in the box over the stove.'

'You deal with that, Tracy. Reckon I should go now.' Chris clearly wanted to be off. 'Get back to the camp while the going's good.'

'Okay. I'll stay here for a while.' Tracy had taken down the tin of tea. 'Got to make sure this stubborn old fella's all right before I get back. Could you ring my uncle when you get across?' She wrote her phone number on a piece of rough paper she found on Jim's table. 'They'll be worried.'

'Sure.' Chris glanced at the note before stuffing it into his shorts pocket. 'I'll tell him you're okay.' He gave her a wink.

After he'd gone, Tracy made tea and poured a mug for Jim. He sat up, produced his bottle of rum and poured some into the dark liquid.

'Pain gone?' she asked.

'Almost.' He waved his mug. Grinned. 'This'll fix it.'

'Well, you're just going to lie right there for now. Get some sleep.' Tracy didn't like the look of the old man. 'I still think you should have a doctor check you out.' And before Jim could open his mouth, she added, 'We'll argue about that in the morning.' She wasn't going to tell him that she'd asked Chris to alert the hospital.

'There's a sleeping bag under the bed.' Jim was obviously sleepy now.

'Don't you worry about me,' Tracy said, removing his mug. 'I'm a big girl now.'

'You are too.' Jim gave a quiet kind of half chuckle and lay back.

When she was sure he was asleep, Tracy sat on, watching the rise and fall of the artist's chest. She listened to his breathing and prayed there would soon be a boat carrying a medic. In spite of being the 'big girl' now, she knew she couldn't deal with this on her own.

45

Having given the police their names, the surfers, Mac and Steve moved off quietly. Now their anger had abated, they became silent. Subdued. They passed by Jim's shack and onto the beach only glancing at it. There was the glow of a lamp, which doubtless indicated all was well. There was no sign of Tracy, so Steve assumed she'd gone back to the mainland. His one thought was to get home and to bed. Tomorrow was another work day. Even in the car, the two men spoke little.

As Mac pulled on the brake and turned off the motor, he turned to Steve. 'Told you I thought those surfing guys could be trouble.' He sighed and yawned.

Steve didn't know what to say.

Then Mac said, 'Guess we should be grateful we came home in one piece.'

'Reckon some of those guys weren't so lucky.'

They both chuckled.

Then Mac added, 'But it wasn't seriously funny, mate, was it? Could have been really bad for old Jim. For us all.'

'Not surprising the mining guys were furious.'

'A stupid idea of the surfers.'

Both Mac and Steve now realised what a terrible act of vandalism had been committed.

Mac sighed and opened the door of his ute. 'Not much we can do about it now,' he said. 'But not a word to Bessie, mate. Don't want the olds to know we were involved unless they have to.'

Steve lay on his bed in the bunkhouse and went over the incident. How bloody stupid it had been. Behaving like kids, his father would say. And for once he would have been right. He remembered Jim standing his ground and telling the surfers that what they were doing was wrong. How they hadn't wanted to listen. Tracy and Chris had taken on getting the old man back to his shack. Where was Tracy now, he wondered. Had she got home safely? Holy shit! Maybe she hadn't! Was still over there with Jim! He hadn't even bothered to check. But it had all looked all right, hadn't it? But maybe it wasn't. Maybe Jim was really bad. But then he'd have gone to hospital, wouldn't he? But how would he get there? Steve's thoughts went round and round. He knew he wouldn't sleep.

After what seemed an age, he got up, flung on the shorts he'd had on before. Noticed some blood on them. There were no lights on now in the farmhouse. He took his bike from its usual position leaning against the wall outside the bunkhouse door. He pedalled down the road towards town again. Wasn't sure what he was expecting to find. Just knew he had to get back into town.

46

At two o'clock in the morning, Tracy finally went down to the beach with the ambulance men. Saw Jim lifted into the boat. Rode with the ambo crew back into town.

Jim was already breathing into an oxygen mask. He didn't look good. Tracy held his hand as the boat sped through the water.

'You've done the right thing, girl,' one of the men said. 'Hospital care is what he needs now.'

Jim clearly had no idea what was going on but seemed reluctant to let go of her hand when he was lifted into the ambulance.

'You'll be right now. I'll be in to see you tomorrow,' she said, but doubted she'd manage it.

She watched the ambulance speed off down the main street and around the corner towards Coffs. She went to where her bike was still in its rack.

An arm went around her shoulders. Strong. Hairy. She gasped before another hand went over her mouth.

She fell back. His body warmth enveloped her as she was dragged somewhere. She wasn't sure where. Then down into the bushes and dirt. She barely noticed the piercing of the little branches as he pushed her down. She struggled, lashed out with her knees, her arms.

He lay on top of her, pushed his hand tighter over her mouth. 'Now, girlie.' He spoke in a kind of hoarse whisper. 'Let's see what's going on inside that tight little cunt.'

With his free hand, he lifted her skirt ripped at her briefs, then entered her. Fear and anger overrode the pain, the burning walloping. It seemed to go on for ever.

Then, suddenly, it was over. He stood up. She wondered if he'd kill her but she didn't matter to him any more. He just wanted to be gone.

She lay still. Watched his figure depart. Disappear into the darkness. Slowly, she forced her sluggish brain to think about where he'd been, where it hurt most.

When she was sure she was still capable of moving, she sat up. Was conscious of the back of her head, where it had been pushed into the dirt. Her whole body felt one big bruise. And she was cold. So cold she was shivering. She struggled to get up. Move away.

Bicycle wheels!

'Holy shit! Trace! What happened?' Steve flung his bike down onto the road, where the wheels continued to spin. He bent down to see her clearly.

She reached out a hand and he took it, helping her to stand. Words wouldn't come from her. Then his arms were round her. She felt the warm softness of his body.

Only then did she cry. Deep sobs from somewhere within. Her tears mixed with her snot as she was enveloped. She didn't care any more.

Steve didn't need to ask what had happened. Her sobs said it all.

'We should go to the police,' he said.

'No.' Tracy hiccupped. 'I know what happens if you tell them.'

'But we should still go,' he said. 'That bastard can't just get away with this.'

She broke from him angrily. Glared at him. 'So you want to see me have to go over it all in public bit by bit, do you?'

'It wouldn't be like that, Tracy.'

'Yes, it would. That's exactly what happens. They make you relive the whole thing. Bully you for details.' She was beginning to cry again. 'And I couldn't face that. I just couldn't.'

'Okay, okay,' Steve said. 'We'll let it go.' He thought, just for now...'

'You men don't get it.' She spoke through her tears. 'And my uncle won't either. It'll be my fault probably.' She looked Steve in the eye. 'And Jim's in hospital. Think he might have had a heart attack but I'm not sure.'

'Oh, shit! Don't worry, Trace. I'll go see him. Make sure he's okay,'

Steve said. 'Probably fine by now.' He felt inadequate. Didn't know what else to say.

But Tracy was angry now. 'Don't think I wouldn't like to see Andy go to jail. Nothing I'd like better. See him squirm.' Her eyes held Steve's. 'But it's his word against mine. Unless I go to a doctor. And he'll only say he can prove I had sex. Not who it was.'

'But it's not fair, Tracy.'

'Who said anything about being fair? Not much is ever fair.'

Steve searched for a response to that. Couldn't really find one. Reached into his pocket for a handkerchief. Realised it was too grubby to wipe her tears. He could only hold her against him. Stroke her back.

After a minute or two, she broke away. 'I think I could manage to get on your bike.' She looked up at him. Spoke in a small voice as though all the fight had gone out of her. 'In front. If you padded it a bit somehow.'

Steve took off his T-shirt and wound it around the crossbar, making a kind of cushion. Very gingerly, she sat sideways and folded one arm onto Steve's waist. He found the extra weight harder than he'd expected but pedalled on, only stopping when he reached the farm, where she slid off and he lent the bike against the wall of the bunkhouse. Wordlessly, he opened the door, switched on the light and led her in.

She briefly looked around his room. 'It's good,' was all she said, before curling up in a foetal position on the bed so she faced the wall.

Steve noticed the blood on her skirt but made no comment.

He didn't bother with anything but kicked off his shoes, switched off the light and slid in beside her, putting one arm around her. There was nothing he could say, but he listened for sounds of her breathing. Believed she wasn't crying now. Figured the only thing he could do was let her know he cared.

47

In the early hours of the morning Steve unwound himself. Stiff from lying in the same position, he lay for a moment listening for the sound of Tracy's breathing. A sign that she was asleep. He could not hear anything so sat up to bend over her.

She was still lying in the curled foetal position with her eyes open.

'Are you okay?' he asked.

She rolled over to face him. 'I'm okay,' she said.

Steve thought she still looked pale but wasn't really sure, as he hadn't seriously looked at her closely much before.

'Mind if I use your bathroom?' she said as she sat up.

'In there.' He jerked his head in the direction of the door.

Steve lay listening to the sound of the shower. It seemed a long time followed by an even longer period of silence. Finally, the door opened and Tracy emerged.

'Better get home,' she said. 'Could you tell Bert I'm sick?'

'Course.'

There was dirt on her T-shirt. Steve thought she looked somehow smaller. Like a kid.

'You going to tell them?'

'Nah,' she said. 'No point. They'd make me go to the cops. Not doing that.'

'I reckon you should.'

It wasn't the right thing to say, he realised.

'You're just another bloke, though, aren't you?' Her anger was immediate and obvious. 'Just another fucking bastard.'

'Hang on, Tracy. You don't need to get…'

'But I am. Very bloody angry. And why shouldn't I be? You guys just go out and bash each other about when you're angry but girls aren't supposed to do that. We aren't strong enough, anyway. But I'd love to smash Andy's face in. Would if I could. The only thing you guys have got going for you is strength, so I wouldn't win even if I had the chance. Still, I'm not going to be Miss Nice Girl. Not any more. I'm not now anyway. Now, I'm that dirty girl. That slutty girl. But I'll tell you this, for what it's worth: there's other ways to kick a guy than with feet or smash a face in with fists. And from here on, I shall use them, Steve. So thanks for the bed and the kind words but you can stick them. I'm looking after me from here on.'

She opened the door to the bunkhouse as she spoke and went out slamming it behind her. Steve had stood and now moved to follow her but thought better of it. How she was going to get home he didn't know. He figured she'd manage somehow. She was angry enough to ignite a fire. But he felt a sadness that she was so angry with him. He hadn't meant to make things worse but he was certain now that he had.

48

If Mac or his parents noticed anything the previous night or had seen Tracy leave the farm, they didn't comment.

'Thank God we got there in time to stop those guys doing anything worse,' were Mac's only words next morning.

'You young 'uns don't know when to leave things alone,' his father said, glancing up from his bacon and eggs.

Steve was concerned to speak to his father before the story spread. Bob Hastings hated negative publicity.

He cycled into town and went to the phone booth, which was hot and sweaty even at eight in the morning. The money clunked into the box.

'Hi, Dad.'

'How are you going, son?' The tone of his father's voice the last few days still surprised Steve.

'Wondering if you're coming up this way today?'

'I had planned to. Why?'

'I'll tell you when you get here. Nothing serious.' No doubt Bob would think it was extremely serious but Steve hoped he could ameliorate the incident in the telling.

'There are certainly things going on here that I hope you're not involved in.'

'Like what?'

'A bloody protest march. That's what. Apparently, the students at the nearby tech college have been listening to the local radio and are all fired up over your little island.'

'It's not my island, Dad. It belongs to everyone.' Steve felt elated that guys and chicks of his age were not only aware of what was happening but also cared. 'That's why they're marching.'

'Well, I'd better be on my way, anyway. The main road could be blocked. Stupid bloody kids.'

'See you, Dad.' Useless to argue with the old man. 'I finish at eleven and don't have to go back till three thirty today. We could have lunch maybe?'

'Going home today,' Bob said. 'Can't leave your mother alone any longer. She's been really upset.'

'I know, Dad. I'm sorry.'

'Well, I'll see you. For a bit. Eleven, you say?'

'Yes. See you then.'

Steve was glad his father was going home if only because he'd no longer feel that he had to explain himself. Account for his actions. He kept thinking with excitement of the protest march. Wouldn't Jim be pleased? Jim! He found some more coins and searched through the remains of the dog-eared and torn phone directory. The page listing Coffs Harbour Base Hospital was still there. Just.

A woman's voice sounded impersonal, efficient. 'Can I help you?'

'I'm wondering how Mr Masters is.'

'Are you a relative?'

'No, just a friend.'

There was short pause.

Then she asked, 'Which ward is he in?'

'I don't know. He only came in last night.'

'Probably still in Casualty. I'll put you through.'

Eventually, another woman's voice. Probably a nurse, Steve thought. 'Yes?'

'I'm wondering how Mr Masters is? Jim Masters. The artist…'

'Who's speaking?'

'I'm a close friend, Steve Markham.'

'He's satisfactory, Mr Markham. He's about to be taken up to a ward. You can visit him between ten and twelve or three and eight today.'

What did satisfactory mean? Could be anything. But if Jim was going to a ward, it meant he wasn't too bad, surely. Maybe his father would take him to see the artist. On his way south. But he wouldn't be the only person to worry about Jim. He'd see Madge before he went to the newsagency.

'I just rang the hospital,' he said later as he entered the shop.

Madge was bent over the ice cream refrigerator.

'Jim's okay, apparently.'

'I only just heard about last night,' she said. 'Silly young louts.' She puffed out. 'And you should know when to leave well alone, young man. Coulda got yourself seriously hurt. Jim shoulda had more sense too. At his age…'

'I'll go to see him later if my dad will take me,' Steve said to mollify her.

'And so you should. Encouraging an old man to fight.' She still had her pouter-pigeon look. 'With fists too, I heard. Might be all right for someone young. But he's too frail to bash men about. Or be bashed.'

Steve could see Madge was thoroughly wound up. He prepared himself for a further tirade. But suddenly she stopped. Went behind the till and pulled out a packet of Drum tobacco.

'You'd better take this to him.' She put it into a paper bag and added a couple of packets of cigarette papers. 'He won't be allowed it in the ward but it'll drive him to get up and go outside.' She chuckled as she handed it to Steve. 'Better in no time when he sees this.'

49

Mick Stuart was in for a worrying day. He could tell. First, his wife had harangued him about their friends who were going off on a cruise in Greece. She wanted to go too. With or without him, she'd said. His mates would have fun with it if she went off on her own. Now, he was facing the problem of the protest march.

That bloody artist! Mick remembered him now. He was behind this. Him and that know-all kid. Going on about the animals and plants. Mick snorted at the memory. His role was to keep the constituents happy, and they wanted more jobs. Jobs made the world go round. His own included. It was logical…pragmatic – he liked that word – to focus on keeping things ticking over. The future was unpredictable. You couldn't go worrying about what might happen in five years' time. Jump each hurdle as you came to it. That's what his father had said. That was the way life functioned. Always had.

The phone rang.

Samantha said, 'The Minister for the Environment to speak to you, sir.'

Shit! This was all getting to be bigger than Ben Hur. Maybe he should go on that cruise. Get away.

'Yes, Bob? How are things down in the big smoke?'

'Parliament sits again in two weeks and I'd like to get the fuss about Sandhill sorted. What's going on?'

'Oh, it's not such a big problem really. All under control, Bob.'

'That's not what the papers say. They make it sound big. Doesn't look good, Mick.'

He swallowed. Pity he couldn't start the day again. 'I don't think many students marched.'

167

'It's not the students I'm worried about, Mick. It's all those others. The flag wavers. The bloody greenies. Lefties. The PM doesn't like them having one bit of publicity. And the papers are giving them plenty.'

'I'll get onto it.' Mick could only think of his own position. Felt sick. Could go to the wall for this, if he didn't handle it well. Wished he could crawl under his desk till it all went away. 'Vice chancellor of the university is a friend of mine. He'll be with me on this. Get the students to stop and the others will too. Like an army without the foot soldiers.' He laughed at his own comparison.

But Bob was less impressed. 'See what you can do, will you? I won't move on this till late this afternoon.'

Holy shit! He'd have to get a move on.

'Should give you time to get something sorted. Right?'

'Sure.'

Mick only knew the vice chancellor slightly. Had met him at some cocktail shindig after a graduation. He tried to remember the occasion. Had the bloke seemed approachable? University had never been Mick's thing. He'd always believed he could sell ice cream to the Eskimos. His strength lay in salesmanship. Now he'd have to seriously use it if he was to keep his nose clean in the PM's eyes.

The vice chancellor was almost as uncooperative as he'd feared. 'Democracy is the name of the game here, Mr Stuart. Short of an absolute insurrection, we allow them to do whatever they feel is necessary. I'm sure you'd be the first to agree that that is as it should be.'

'Of course.' Mick found his best voice and speech. Important to sound well educated. 'I'm just concerned that we don't give the anti-mining lobby too much encouragement. It's jobs that we're keen to promote. Something that must surely concern your students. Their futures.' He allowed a pause so the words could penetrate.

'I'll let the student body know.' The vice chancellor still sounded remote. 'I'll even go so far as to tell them they are misguided in this.'

The bastard's tone was almost patronising. Bloody stuck-up academic.

He'd have to talk to the coppers. And the local newspapers. Make sure the journos got the proper story. He mentally wrote the headline. 'Students destroy opportunity.' He'd have to get this all sorted before four o'clock. Time to show the PM that he had the electorate totally with him on this. There was a sour taste in his mouth. He guessed his breath must be bad.

50

Next day, Tracy told her olds she had been with Mel. She phoned to warn her friend. 'Cover for me, would you? If the old people ask, that is.'

Mel laughed. 'Course. 'Bout time you broke free. Who is he?'

'Nobody you'd know.' For a second, she thought tears would rise. She fought them down.

'Try me. Bet I would.'

Tracy spoke gently. 'Secret just now. Might tell you one day.'

She rang Bert to say she'd be late in. A migraine. One more lie. All the rules were broken now.

How could she act normally when her world had been tipped on its head? Fear and disgust had replaced certainty and security. Part of her ached to tell a friend. But the other part told her to keep it to herself. Only Steve need ever know. Like when her parents had been killed, Tracy knew that the memories of most hurts fade with time. She had tried to hang on to what she remembered of her mother and father but so much had become dimmed. Like peering through steam. This awfulness would gradually lose itself too. Become muddled. But she'd never forget the smell of him.

She needed someone to talk to. Steve! He was the only one who knew. But she'd been so angry. Not with him. Just with the horror of it. The sticky wet. Her aunt was out when she got home so she'd showered and showered. Sat on the tiles, her tears mixing with the water. Had thrown away her skirt. Bundled it up and shoved it to the bottom of the rubbish bin. Covered it up with kitchen waste. She'd read somewhere that deep breathing helped things. She tried to mentally count her breaths. In and out. In and out.

170

Trying to be her usual self was hardest. It must be written all over her. On her face, in her eyes. Dirty girl. And what if she met Andy? He wouldn't say anything, though. Would he? Might tell another bloke. Then word would get around. Tracy's a slut. An easy lay.

When she eventually went in to work, she couldn't eye the men in the face. Looked at the beer glasses, the ashtrays, the coasters on the bar. If Andy was there, she didn't see him. Bert was his usual self. In some strange way, he helped her keep going. The normalness of him. His gruff solidity. It was all a haze and she was on autopilot most of the time.

In the middle of supper, she looked at the mince on her plate and felt sick. Ran from the room. Threw up in the toilet.

'Better stay home tomorrow, Trace.'

'I'll be fine tomorrow.'

And she would be. As fine as she'd ever be. Nothing would ever be the same again.

51

Steve's farewell with his father took place just outside the hospital, a large red-brick forbidding building. Bob pulled into the kerb and Steve opened the door. Hesitated. Turned back to his father. He felt awkward. Annoyed with himself and with the old man. He hoped there wasn't going to be a scene.

He grinned in a gritted teeth kind of way. 'Give my love to Mum. Tell her I'm fine. Dunno exactly when I'll be back home.'

'We've both given up on that idea,' his father said without rancour. 'We just wonder what we did wrong. Thought we'd given you the perfect start to life.'

'I guess you did, Dad.' Steve struggled to find a way to put this. 'I just don't want what you want. At least, not what you want for me.'

'Well, it's not too late, son. You could still have a good career in something useful.' There was a wistful plea in his father's voice.

Steve felt a momentary sense of guilt. Then he managed a forced laugh. 'See you, Dad,' He swung out of his seat, slammed the door shut behind him and stood upright on the footpath. He looked down at his father before giving a final wave.

The car slid out into the road.

Inside the hospital foyer, Steve was greeted by an antiseptic smell and bright artificial light. A patient with relatives wandered by, pushing a still-attached drip bag.

The receptionist was on the phone but hung up when Steve approached. She smiled. 'Can I help you?'

Jim was on the third floor and he took the lift as directed. He reflected that even if he'd been blindfolded, he would have known this was a hospital by the smells and sounds mixed with the sense of busy efficiency. His sandshoes squeaked on the polished lino floor. Before he reached the nurses' station, he saw Jim's form in the second room along the corridor. The old man was on his back, head propped up on pillows, his mouth half open.

As Steve approached the bed, Jim opened his eyes. They were warm pools of blue.

'Hello, son,' he said, his voice frail, his body shrunken.

'Hi.' Steve felt embarrassed. Inadequate. What did one say to a sick man? 'Thought I'd come in,' he said with forced brightness. 'How are you?' Silly question.

Jim gave one of his half smiles. 'Was just thinking about you,' he said. 'Your old man still here?'

'Just left. Why?'

'Pity. I'd have liked to meet him.' Jim coughed and his whole body contorted. For a few seconds, he fought for breath. 'Wanted to talk to him about your art. Your talent.'

'I don't really have talent.' Steve was embarrassed again. The old man could see through him. 'Not specially.'

Jim ignored that. 'Just thought he should know. Might understand you ought to use that. The gift.'

'Maybe.' Steve could see that talking tired Jim. Felt he should go.

'University's not for you,' Jim went on almost as though talking to himself. His voice was suddenly stronger. 'Go to art school. Learn how to paint properly. You've no idea. Not yet.'

Indignation rose but Steve stopped himself from giving voice to it.

'It's there,' Jim added. 'It's there. You just need to learn how to use it.' He gave another of his half smiles. 'You young uns think you know it all.' His eyes closed. 'But you'll find out. Given time.' His voice was becoming weaker. 'You've got plenty of that.'

There was a pause. For some reason, Steve lingered.

Jim's eyes suddenly opened again. 'Where's the girl?'

'Tracy?'

'Yes. Good kid. Stayed with me, you know. Got the ambulance. I'd like to thank her.'

Steve patted the old man's hand. It was thin and dry like paper. 'I'll tell her,' he said and saw the old man's eyes had closed again. 'You should rest now. I'll come again,' he said.

But Jim's breathing was shallow and he seemed already asleep.

52

She should apologise to Steve. He'd done his best. Helped her. But he was fixated on the police. As if they were the cure-all. They weren't. While Tracy worried over what had happened and what she should do, she knew the police weren't an option.

'You okay, Trace?' Bert sounded and looked concerned.

She would have loved to confide in him but could just imagine his response. She could only say, 'I'm okay, thanks.'

'You feeling all right?' her aunt asked more than once.

She knew she must look sick. Pale, at least. 'I'm fine,' she lied. 'Just that time of the month.' That always put an end to questions. Women's hormones were secret. Shameful almost.

At around ten o'clock, she saw Steve go down to Madge's shop. Her chance.

'Can I go down to Madge's?'

'Your daily chocolate milk?' Bert clicked his tongue in mock disapproval. Gave a chuckle. He knew her ways.

Steve had just paid Madge and was carrying his Coke to sit at one of the little tables outside.

She deliberately blocked his path out the door. 'Hi,' she said, embarrassed but trying to look friendly.

'Hi. You okay?' His eyes were concerned.

His smell of soap and aftershave momentarily wiped away the memory of Andy's sweat and stale beer.

'I'm okay. Could we go somewhere to talk?' She spoke hesitantly.

'Got to be back at work in a minute. Sorry.'

'This evening?' She didn't want the moment to pass.

'Okay. Meet you outside the pub. What time you finishing?'

'Six.' Tracy managed a smile.

'See you there.'

They were still standing in the doorway. Both reluctant to go.

'Yeah. See you,' she echoed.

Then she turned to go back to the pub and he went towards the newsagency. He looked back at her before he went inside. She gave him a little wave. Each carried the other in their minds. The warm glow of sharing.

53

'Thing is, Mick,' Bert perched on his bar stool, 'thing is, I got bookings for this place for weeks now. And the van park's jam-packed.' Bert had met Mick Stuart several times. Didn't think much of him but he was the pollie they'd got.

'Well, I'm not here about that. It's the bloody students, the commie little bastards, that worry me. They're up in arms about the bloody mining. That fucking little island. What's it called?'

Sandhill.'

'Nobody much goes there, I heard.'

'They didn't. Do now but.'

'Why's that?'

'Ever since that business with the sand mining lot. Put the place on the map. Got a good surfing beach. The young uns don't like the idea of anyone stuffing it up. Had a bit of a showdown about it.' Bert chuckled. 'Place has become a kind of a surfing legend for 'em.'

'But would it still attract people if the mine folded? That's what you got to ask yourself.'

Bert thought for a moment. 'Reckon. It's caught on, see. And once a place has become known, there's nothing much can be done to change it. Course they try to catch a glimpse of the old artist. Jim. He's a bit of a hero now. His idea to speak up against the mining. Thinks the island is special. Not sure why meself. But I'm not an artist.' He chuckled again. 'Not a surfer either, but the old artist, Jim, loves the place. Had an exhibition of his paintings of the island. Said he wanted people to know how beautiful the place is. Been livin' there himself a few years.'

'I gather he's famous. As an artist, that is.'

'His paintings sell for a tidy sum is all I know. Don't understand 'em meself. He was injured in the punch-up.' Bert looked around for Tracy. 'Me bar girl, Tracy, looked after him. Got him into hospital.'

'Any charges laid?' The more he heard about it, the more Mick Stuart wished the whole issue would just go away. Get the minister off his back.

'I gather there were but I dunno who or what's happening about it.'

'Any miners charged?'

'Nah. Don't think so. They'd say they was defending their property. Probably were too. Things just got a bit out of hand.'

'Well, I can tell you the minister isn't too pleased with the news. Made the city papers. Big time. I think he's maybe going to come up to see for himself. If it gets any worse, that is. D'you think it'll blow over now?'

'Might… Then again, it might not.'

'Perhaps I need to talk to the college students.' This idea didn't appeal.

'Maybe. But I'd let it ride for a bit. Things have a habit of sorting themselves.' Bert's usual philosophy. 'Like a beer?'

Mick Stuart nodded and, as he watched the brown liquid flow into his glass, he reflected that it might be a good night to get thoroughly pissed.

54

Steve and Tracy walked down towards the wharf. They hadn't decided. It just seemed the natural place to go. Most of the boats seemed to be out and only one or two bobbed on their moorings. They sat with their feet dangling over the edge of the timber pier.

For a few seconds, neither of them spoke. Then they both spoke together.

'Sorry I was…'

'I should have…'

They laughed.

'You haven't told anyone, have you?' Tracy asked, her eyes searching Steve's face.

'Nah. You said not to.' He grinned. 'I do as I'm told.'

'Bet you don't most of the time.'

'This wasn't most of the time,' he said and his eyes were serious. 'This was really bad. Like nothing I thought would happen.' There was another pause and Tracy looked down. 'You okay now?'

'I'm okay. Thanks for taking me back to yours. Couldn't have gone home.'

'Well, you didn't have to get angry with me. I only wanted to help.'

'I had to get angry with someone. Anyone. Sorry.'

'Are you still?'

'Angry with you?' She swung her legs. Looked at him and smiled. 'Nah. You're just a kid.'

'I'm not.' He stared at her indignantly. 'Even the old man has discovered that.

Tracy ran a hand up and down his arm. 'Just teasing,' she said.

'Well, don't.'

179

For answer, she flung both arms round his neck and drew him to her. He remained stiff and unyielding. Then their lips met. It was some time before the silence was broken.

Steve finally stood up. 'Let's go,' he said.

'I need a phone booth,' Tracy said. 'Let them know I'm with a friend.'

'Male or female?' He grinned at her.

There was another pause as they kissed again.

'Reckon you're all male,' she said and laughed. 'But you'll be female to my uncle and aunt.'

When she'd made the call, she took her bike down from the rack and he pulled his from where he always left it against the wall of the newsagency. If Joe saw him, he pretended not to.

They cycled together back to the bunkhouse. There seemed to be nobody about at the homestead. One of the dogs barked, but nobody came outside.

Steve discovered how to gently make love in the growing dark of the bunkhouse.

55

'What you got planned for the future?' Tracy was sitting up in bed, her knees drawn up under her chin. Steve still lay beside her. 'Like for work.'

He looked up at her. 'Dunno,' he said, before dragging her down to lie with him.

After they had made love again, she pushed him gently away and sat up.

'But you can't go on working at Joe's. Not forever.'

'And are you going to go on working at the pub forever?'

'No, I'm not. Can't stay in this town either. He's here. Not sure if I can do what I want, though.'

'What's that?'

Tracy laughed. 'Ask no questions and you'll be told no lies. I'm working on it.'

'Well, good luck with that.' Steve was miffed that she wouldn't tell him. They'd just made love, for god's sake.

'No need to sulk. I promise you'll be the first to know if my plans get the go ahead.' She had her head on one side, a questioning look. 'And you haven't said what your plans are.'

Steve rolled over on his back to look at her. 'I don't think Dad will like what I want.'

'Not his life, though, is it?'

'No,' he laughed and sat up so his eyes were level with hers. 'I guess we're both kind of free to do what we like.'

She stared back at him, unsmiling now. 'But we mustn't give in to other things.'

'You mean, sex or…or falling in love.'

'Suppose. We both oughta do something sensible first…like have a career.'

'Why should we be sensible?'

'Because if we aren't, we'll be sorry later.' Her eyes wandered as she thought about it. 'I want to know I can do something different. Prove it to myself. Be someone other than Tracy, that girl who works in the pub.'

'You are someone different. To me anyway.'

'You know what I mean.' She slid off the bed and stood up. 'Right now, I'm gunna have a shower and get back to town.' She laughed. 'To the pub I don't want to work in any more.'

Steve sat staring at the door, absorbing her words while the shower ran.

'All yours,' she said when she came out of the bathroom. She gave him a kiss and he tried to grab her but she evaded him and made for the door. 'See you,' she said and was gone.

He showered and dressed slowly while he digested the past hours. When he got into town, he went to the phone booth and dialled his father. No point in putting things off.

56

The news, when it was relayed by Bert, caused a few muted cheers mixed with groans in the pub. Bert initially felt a sense of relief tinged with concern that it might not auger well for the town in the long run.

One of the suited mining men had come in half an hour before. 'We're pulling out,' he said. 'Sorry to disappoint.'

'Why's that?' Bert was at a loss to immediately understand.

'Found somewhere else more suitable.' The man looked relaxed and sounded quite cheerful. 'On the mainland. Further north. You'll read about it, no doubt.'

'So Sandhill's gunna be left as it is then. After all that?'

'Yes. And I can't say we'll be sorry. Too difficult to get all the equipment across. Too expensive.'

One of the locals muttered over the bar to Bert, 'Too much fuss, I reckon.'

It was on the tip of Bert's tongue to say the surfers would be pleased but he didn't want to trigger antagonism.

There had been other news that gave him food for thought. Madge had been in briefly during one of her short breaks. Nowadays, she had to have a back-up. Everyone had become busier.

'Might give up the shop,' Madge had said. 'Might have to.'

'Why's that?'

'I heard a whisper some company's setting up a big grocery place down the road. Near the camping grounds, I was told. Couldn't compete with that.'

A pause while Bert took in her words. She was a fixture in the town. Like his pub.

'Could diversify, Madge.' He'd recently learned that word and what it meant. 'You could go in for clothes or…or…' Bert had one of his ideas, '…or surfing gear. Something like that.'

Madge had glared at him, snorted and stumped off. But he knew she'd be thinking about it. She'd be pleased with the latest news.

For the moment anyway, the town wasn't going to miss the mining company.

'Struth! That Mick Stuart must be heaving a sigh of relief.

57

At just past eleven, the ambulance stopped outside the pub. It had made a couple of other stops along the way but this time it sat for a while to let the last passenger, an elderly man, out.

'You sure you'll be okay?' the ambulance man asked. 'How you getting the last bit home?'

'I'll be fine. One of the fishing blokes'll give me a ride.' Jim hated fuss.

He stood for a while, savouring the smell of the place. Feeling the warmth of the sun on his face. He had only the things Tracy had flung in his bag. He wore the same clothes he had gone to hospital in and they had made him feel at home before he actually got there.

He called in at Madge's shop before going down to the wharf. 'Thanks for the tobacco,' he said, touching his forehead in a kind of salute.

'T'weren't no trouble, Jim.' Madge's smile lit up her face. 'Good to see you back. D'you need anything to take back with you? Bread? Milk?'

'Might have a loaf and some more tobacco.' Jim wanted to be back on the island. Felt a bit wobbly now.

Down on the jetty, he found Custer, who said he'd take him across.

'Where you been?' the fisherman asked. 'Thought you hadn't been around for a while.'

'Been in hospital. Big fuss at the mining site. Leg still a bit dodgy but I'll be fine when I get home.'

Custer had heard all about the fight. Now, he covertly studied Jim. Thought the old man looked frailer than ever. The tendons on his neck were taut, flesh sunk in between. When he reached up to help the artist down into the boat, the skin of the old man's hand was dry and paper-

185

thin. Old age had a dehydrating effect, he thought. He was gentler than usual and when they got to the other side, he took the boat in as far as he dared before hopping out to help the artist.

'She'll be right.' Jim slithered over the side and into the cool water. The feel of his feet on the pebble-strewn sand was another joyful moment. He turned to watch Custer start the motor and turn the boat. Gave a salute of thanks.

Each blade of grass along the little path to his shack seemed to reach out to him in welcome. The birds screeched and darted among the trees. The sunlight made patterns through the leaves. Jim felt tears bubble. Cursed himself. No sentimentality now. But God, it was good to be back.

In the shack, he filled and put on a kettle. Reminded himself to buy another bottle of gas. Reached into the hidey-hole for his bottle of brandy. He knew he was getting weaker now. Should be lying down. But it was all too wonderful to leave just yet.

Carrying his cup of coffee, he went outside to sit in his usual spot. Pulled out his tobacco and papers and slowly made a cigarette. He absorbed every sound and smell as though for the first time. What a marvellous place. He'd forgotten, even in a week, just how lucky he was to be a part of this paradise.

He lit his cigarette at last. Sat on in the glowing light. Watched the smoke curl up towards the ferns clumped around the little dwelling. The brandy-infused coffee was warm and he inwardly smiled. Perfection with each mouthful.

58

They were sitting on the jetty, arms around each other, feet dangling over the edge.

Tracy pulled away to look Steve in the face. 'So, have you decided anything yet?'

'Reckon I have. You?'

'Yes.'

There was silence for a few seconds.

'Aren't you going to ask me what?'

'S'pose so.'

'Gunna go to the big smoke.'

'To do what?'

'Try nursing.' Before he could comment, she added, 'What I've often dreamed about. Always wanted to do. I just wasn't sure I could. Dunno why, really.'

'I reckon anyone can do pretty much anything if they're brave enough.'

'I got the form to fill out. Came in the mail yesterday.' She stared out to sea. 'It is kind of scary but I think I can do it. My aunt and uncle were really nice about it. Enthusiastic even. A bit of a surprise.'

'Probably keen to see you gone,' Steve grinned and she gave him a shove. 'Watch out! I could fall in.'

'Serve you right if you did.' There was silence for another few seconds. 'So tell me your plans.'

'I'm going to go to art school.' It sounded exciting, even as he said the words. 'Rang Dad last night. We talked.' Steve now stared out to sea as though lost in thought. 'We actually talked like adults. He said if that was what I wanted, then I should go ahead.'

'Is it easy to get in? Is it expensive?'

'It could be expensive. Depends where I go. But the old man actually said he'd pay. I can't believe it. Not how things used to be with him.'

'Why d'you think he's changed like that?'

'He said he knows now what he's up against.' Steve laughed. 'Says I'm like my sister. They used to argue he says, but they don't now. Course she's become the big success story. Making lots of money. He likes that. Reckons I'll never make a cent. Says artists don't. Not unless they're like Jim.'

'Jim!' Tracy stood up. We should go see if he's all right. Tell him how things are.'

'Okay.' Steve stood beside her.

'There's another thing,' she said.

'Yes. What?'

'Remember what I said about not letting things stand in the way of a career?'

'Sort of. You said something about not letting other things take over, or get sidetracked or something.'

'Well…' She looked serious and Steve knew what she was trying to say.

'So you're telling me I'm getting you sidetracked?'

'Not at the moment. But you could. I could do the same to you.'

'So you're saying…' he paused, his eyes on hers, 'you don't want to…to…go on like this?'

She smiled at him in, he thought, an I'm-an adult-you're-not kind of way. 'Later, maybe. Right now, we need a bit of space. Let things kinda happen.'

'But we only just got together.'

'And we might get together again but not yet. We've both got things to do.'

Steve both felt and looked disappointed, so she added, 'I want us to go on together too but let's just see how things go. All right?'

'S'pose so.' Why did Tracy seem much older than he was at times?

He knew, in a way, she was right but didn't want to admit it and certainly didn't want her to know how he felt. 'As you said, right now we've got to see Jim.'

They waited a while to hitch a ride but it was warm in the sun and, for the moment, they were together. Steve hoped time would prove she was wrong and they could go on as they were.

After they got off the boat, they waded to shore. They held hands as they walked up the track to Jim's place.

He was sitting in his usual place, his back to them. It looked as though he was staring up at the canopy of green. They called out and waved but he didn't respond. When they came closer, they saw what looked like a little smile of pleasure lingering on his lips.

www.ingramcontent.com/pod-product-compliance
Lightning Source LLC
Chambersburg PA
CBHW021334190726
48288CB00003B/1109